THE PURITAN

Francis Ferriter, an unusual Irishman living in Dublin, feels driven to purify by violence the society in which he lives.

To achieve this aim he ritualistically murders a woman living in the same boarding house as himself during the early hours of a morning because he is convinced she is a drunk and a prostitute.

The effects of this crime are exciting and complex. Liam O'Flaherty's genius ensures that the reader's attention is held until the final pages of the book when Ferriter explains his motives and his philosophy that 'There is no God, but man has a divine destiny.'

THE PURITAN

LIAM O'FLAHERTY

LYTHWAY PRESS LTD
BATH

First published 1932
by
Jonathan Cape Ltd
This edition published
by
Lythway Press Ltd
by arrangement with the copyright holder
1973

SBN 85046 391 2

Printed in Great Britain by
Redwood Press Limited, Trowbridge, Wiltshire
Bound by Cedric Chivers Ltd, Bath

THE PURITAN

CHAPTER I

SHORTLY after midnight on Sunday, June 21st, Francis Ferriter left the offices of the *Morning Star* in O'Connell Street, Dublin, and returned to his lodgings in Lower Gardiner Street.

It was a warm night, yet he wore his raincoat buttoned, with the collar turned up, and he walked in the huddled manner of a person feeling cold. During the previous January he had spent three weeks in a nursing home, owing to a bout of influenza brought on by overwork and insufficient nourishment. Since then he was constantly in dread of catching a chill and believed himself threatened with consumption. This worry about his health, together with the recent misfortune of his family, accentuated the melancholy that follows influenza to such a degree that his mind had become slightly disordered. Two years previously, his father, who had been a prosperous solicitor in the County Cavan, died suddenly, after having gone bankrupt through foolish speculations. Consequently Francis was compelled to give up studying for the bar and become a journalist. Being unfitted by temperament for this profession, he made poor progress at it, and had come to regard himself as a man treated harshly by society.

He was twenty-four years of age, but his illness and anxiety about his career had already brought deep lines into his forehead, hollowed his eyes, and given his whole countenance an expression of acute sadness that was almost terrifying. His face was of a sickly, pale colour, except for two faint patches of red on his high cheekbones. His eyes were brown and very arresting, owing to their fixed and melancholy expression. His mouth was wide, with thin lips. His jaws tilted upwards at the chin and were so highly developed that they protruded, right to the ears, far out over the rest of his head. This gave the impression that his forehead receded abnormally. On the whole, his countenance looked refined and intellectual. He carried himself in the listless manner of a person who has never taken any strenuous exercise, stooping slightly at the shoulders, with hanging head, dragging his feet and moving half sideways, as if eager to avoid unpleasant contacts. His clothes were old and his trousers were frayed on the inside, where his ankles brushed, but he did not look shabby, because of his strange dignity.

He walked slowly, with his eyes on the pavement, until he turned into Lower Gardiner Street from Beresford Place. Then he raised his head and looked around him excitedly.

'Perhaps he has gone early to-night,' he thought, 'and that she has locked her door. If she is in bed alone and I knock, she will either refuse to admit me or else scream when she sees me. Furthermore I might be heard or seen by somebody in the house. If he has gone I'll have to postpone it.'

He shuddered violently and came to a halt.

'Impossible,' he whispered. 'I couldn't endure it for another week.'

He shook his head several times and walked on until he reached the house in which he lived. As he mounted the steps to the door he paused again in order to examine the street, suddenly became nervous lest anybody might have seen him halt and meditate on the pavement; but there was nobody in sight. The long, wide street, once a fashionable thoroughfare and now rapidly degenerating into a slum, stretched empty from the river to Mountjoy Square, two uniform lines of red brick houses, with iron balconies on the upper windows. The gloom of night concealed their shabbiness and they looked dignified as of old.

He unlocked the door gently and entered the hall on tiptoe. He listened. There was no sound in the house. He closed the door, taking great care to make no noise. Then he crept along the hall stealthily. A stream of moonlight was coming through the bull's-eye window at the return of the stairway leading from the rear of the hall to the basement, getting wider until it ended at the umbrella-stand near the door. This made everything as distinct as by day, but of a yellow colour. He paused at the first of two doors that stood on the right. He listened at the keyhole but heard nothing. He listened at the other door. He heard a man and woman whispering. He nodded, straightened himself, threw back his head and smiled. His face, caught by the moonbeams, looked like that of a corpse. Then he walked quietly up the wide stairway until he came to a small white door at the top of the first flight. This door led into the bathroom. He pushed it open, entered, and looked around dreamily. There was a smell of scented soap.

'Somebody may enter while I'm waiting here,' he thought. 'It's the only flaw in my scheme.

But it's not likely at this hour of the night. I must take that risk.'

He left the bathroom and continued to mount the stairs to the top floor. The house grew shabbier as he climbed and there was a heavy, unpleasant smell of disinfectant, which the lodgers used in summer to kill bed bugs. There was carpet on the stairs to the third landing. Thence the stairs became narrower and were merely covered with a narrow strip of ragged linoleum. As he was climbing this last flight, Ferriter paused and remembered that it was exactly at this spot, six weeks previously, he first thought of making the sacrifice of blood. He folded his arms on his chest and began to think, in order to find out why the idea had first come to him at this spot and why he should remember that fact at this moment.

'There are two explanations,' he said to himself at length, 'or rather it is more correct to say that there is a physical as well as a spiritual explanation for it. I remember on that night my sense of hearing was offended by a drunken man using foul language in that room facing the stairs on the third landing. That made the sordidness of this house painfully apparent to me. To-night my sense of smell is offended by the disinfectant used to kill unclean insects. It will be wrong however to suggest that the idea came into my mind because my vanity was humiliated, but right to maintain that my soul rebelled against uncleanliness, which is the symbol of spiritual degradation.'

There were two rooms leading off the top landing, his own and another rented by an insurance agent called Fitzgerald. On the landing itself, a tiny kitchen had been rigged up, with shelves, a sink in which there was a wash-basin, and a small oil-stove. He struck a match and lit a gas jet. Then he lit the oil stove and put a kettle of water on for tea. He was in the habit of doing this every night when he came home from the office and although he did not want tea this evening, he didn't want to change his habits, lest it might arouse suspicion after-wards.

Having put the kettle on the stove and pre-pared a tray for tea, he entered his room. It was quite large, but the roof was so low that he had to crouch in places, where it sloped towards the eaves. The furniture was scant, but in good taste, especially a thick blue carpet, which had been sent to him by his mother, when he was furnishing the room. There was also, on the wall over the mantelpiece, a good copy of the Vision of Saint Francis by El Greco. All round the walls, there were green wooden shelves stacked with books. In an alcove beside his trunk there was a great pile of magazines and newspapers on the floor. Another corner was curtained off as a wardrobe. A large writing desk lay before the window. In the centre of the floor there was a small folding-table of good quality, also a present from his mother. A divan bed and three chairs completed the furniture.

Having changed into his pyjamas and dressing gown, he returned to the landing and made tea, which he brought back to his room. He was going to pour some into a cup, when he jumped to his feet and said, half aloud:

'It's a small matter, but it may be important.'

He went out and knocked at the door of the other room. Fitzgerald, the insurance agent, a tall, dark-haired man in shirt sleeves, opened the door.

'Excuse me,' said Ferriter, 'could I borrow a cigarette from you? I came in without any.'

Fitzgerald fetched a packet, and Ferriter took one. Having thanked the man, he was turning away, when he suddenly said:

'By the way, have you got the right time?

I make it a quarter to one, but I think I'm slow.'

'That's just right,' said Fitzgerald, after looking at his watch.

'Thanks. Good-night. I'm feeling very sleepy to-night.'

He returned to his room and locked the door. Then he drank a cup of tea. Now he was beginning to get nervous. The two faint patches on his cheeks had become bright red and the root of his tongue was getting in the way of his breath. He went over to his desk, sat down, unlocked a drawer and took out some sheets of manuscript that were pinned together. On the title page was written in red ink: 'THE SACRIFICE OF BLOOD by FRANCIS FERRITER'. He toyed with the pages for a little while. Then he lit a reading lamp that stood on the table and pulled the blind over the window. He turned over the title-page and began to read, but ceased after the first sentence and got to his feet, trembling with excitement.

'No, no,' he said aloud. 'It would tire me and make me quite unable to do what I'm going to do. In any case, it's absolutely correct and there's no necessity to revise it. I shall leave it here under this weight.'

He put a paper-weight over the manuscript on the desk.

'If for any reason I fail to execute my purpose or lose my senses afterwards, as is quite possible in my weak condition, I shall be able to prove through this confession the motives that inspired me.'

His agitation had now increased so much that he felt giddy. He sat down in the chair, covered his face with his hands and began to pray. However, he was unable to form the customary image of God in his mind and he merely repeated words without any fervour. This made him angry and he recovered his self-possession. His jaws set firmly and he remained entirely without thought for a long time, staring at the table. It seemed as if his mind passed slowly downwards into a state of complete oblivion, like death. Then it returned, with the same slowness, in a state of complete unity, being possessed of one idea, which attained such power that it passed down from his mind into his whole body, so that his limbs acted directly in obedience to it, without any guidance from his will. Yet it had no form, either in words or in substance, being symbolized merely by a small cloud of vague colour.

Like a man moving in a dream, he rose from the chair and walked to the wardrobe, where he took a pair of kid gloves from the pocket of his raincoat. He pulled them on slowly and went to the door. As he was unlocking it, the idea suddenly took shape for a few moments and visions of extraordinary vividness flashed through his mind. His body tingled and he had to make a great effort of will in order to prevent himself from shouting and rushing headlong from the room. Then the visions disappeared as suddenly as they had come, and he moved stealthily out of the room, pausing on the landing in order to listen for sounds from his neighbour's room. He heard nothing at first, but after a little while he heard the creaking of a bed, as caused by a man turning in his sleep. He looked at his watch and not being able to read the time, he went back into his room, in order to examine it in the lamplight. He hurried back to his writing desk, found that it was half-past one and then put out the light. Again he left the room and leaving the door open, moved carefully down the stairs in his stockinged feet, carrying his slippers in his hand.

On the second landing he stumbled against the banister as he was rounding the corner. The banister creaked, making a slight noise that seemed thunderous to his excited ears. He stopped dead and his agitation returned. Again the bright red patches came to his cheeks and his tongue lurched against the mouth of his throat. A heaviness spread from his shoulders to his wrists, and his hands became so light that he had to keep rotating them on his wrists. Fearing that he was going to lose control of himself, he hurried down the stairs to the bathroom, careless of what noise he made, hardly drawing breath until he found himself standing within the white door. Now the heaviness in his arms spread to his whole body and he grew panic-stricken, lest he might at the last moment fail to achieve his purpose through physical weakness. In a rage, he set his jaws and made a supreme effort to recover his strength, closing his eyes and throwing back his head until his neck became rigid. This movement made him hold his breath. His face became suffused with bright colour and his nervous tension increased until he was on the point of shouting; but when he reached a point where he thought he could endure the strain no longer, the panic ceased and his mind grew clear. Then he relaxed and began to rehearse what he had to do.

At one point he raised his hand, pointed his finger and said:

'If the knife is not there what am I to do?'

He thought for a few moments and then looked around him wildly.

'Not that way,' he said. 'She might scream. And in any case there would be no blood.'

He shuddered and continued:

'The knife must be there. Otherwise I am wrong and that is obviously impossible. If the knife is not there it means that I have been inspired by the devil acting on my vanity, that I am mad, and that belief in the divine destiny of man is an illusion. This act must be a final solution of the problem — Does God exist?'

Now he began to breathe heavily and to sway backwards and forwards slightly like an intoxicated person. His mind became confused and a sombre enthusiasm, that was almost sensual, made him forget completely where he was and what he was going to do, until he was roused from this ecstasy after twenty minutes by the turning of a door knob down below. In spite of the ecstasy, his senses had remained marvellously acute, for the sound was hardly audible at the distance to the average human ear, yet it reached him loudly and distinctly. He at once became intent, with his head turned sideways, listening.

After a few moments he heard steps in the hallway, followed by a voice whispering 's-s-sh.' Then he heard more footsteps. He counted ten. Then he quickly pulled open the bathroom door and crept out on the stairs. He put on his slippers. The sounds of footsteps were now at the bottom of the stairs leading to the basement. He moved quickly down the stairs, turned to the left and entered by the second door, which was standing ajar. He found himself in a large bedroom. The air was thick with cigarette smoke. There was also a smell of stale beer. From the centre of the ceiling, a large gas chandelier was hanging, surrounded with glass pendants. One of its five lamps was lit. There was a table beneath the chandelier. Several empty Guinness bottles and a half-empty whisky bottle lay on the table, together with two ashtrays laden with cigarette butts. A double bed stretched across the room on the far side of the table. The bedclothes were in disorder, and there were various parts of a woman's underclothing scattered here and there on the floor and on chairs.

After glancing quickly around the room, he moved to a door that led into the front room.

This door was protected by a heavy curtain, hung from a brass rod. He passed behind the curtain, opened the door leading into the front room and walked straight towards the fireplace. On the wall over the mantelpiece an Eastern dagger was hung in a sheath. He steadied the sheath with his left hand and then pulled forth the knife with his right. He ran across the room on tiptoe, pulled the door wide open into the sitting room and hid behind the curtain. Now his face bore an expression of pain, like a man straining to lift a heavy weight. He stood with his shoulders drawn together and his right hand, holding the dagger, raised to the level of his ear. A noise like the ticking of a watch resounded in his head.

He had not been many moments standing behind the curtain when he heard light footsteps in the hall outside and then he moved his head close to a slight opening in the curtain. A woman entered the bedroom, closed the door behind her and turned the key in the lock. Immediately he shuddered and a violent hatred of the woman mounted to his eyes. Then he felt a savage exaltation, which made him clutch the dagger so fiercely that he burst the fastening of his glove. He got ready to spring from behind the curtain, by gripping the folds with his left hand and putting his right foot a little forward.

After locking the door the woman paused for a few seconds, looking at the floor. Then she yawned and stretched her arms above her head. She laced her fingers and then brought down her hands to the back of her neck. Holding her neck between her joined hands, with her elbows close together, she walked swaying towards the table, yawning and frowning. She was a beautiful woman, young, with golden hair and a very fair complexion. She wore a blue silk kimono with white stars, fastened at the waist with a belt, and sandals with green heels. When she reached the table she picked up the whisky bottle as if to pour out a drink, but she put it down again, muttering something. Then she came over to the bed and began to arrange the disordered clothing. The foot of the bed was within two feet of where Ferriter was hiding. When she came to the foot in order to tuck the end of the sheet under the mattress, he decided that the moment had arrived.

Suddenly he swept aside the curtain with his left hand, took deliberate aim at her bended back above the waist and struck with all his might. As he did so, he experienced such a violent exaltation that he grew quite limp as soon as he had struck the blow, loosing the dagger and letting his arm drop to his side. The knife had sunk to the very hilt, finding by chance a clear passage between two ribs straight to the heart. The handle quivered after the blade had become buried and the woman, uttering no sound, fell forward, until she lay straddled across the low rail at the foot of the bed. Then she made a low, rough sound in her throat like a hiccough and her body began to quiver.

Ferriter stood still while her body continued to quiver, entirely devoid of any feeling. Then he heard the squelching sound the dagger had made, and he put his hand to his forehead to allay an acute pain caused by something sharp that seemed to be running around inside his skull. As this pain became more acute, he stepped to one side, leaned forward, took the corpse by the hair and pulled it off the bed on to the floor, where he dropped it face downwards. Then he rubbed his gloved hands together, stared at the corpse and tried to remember what he was to do next. He felt utterly exhausted and could not think. Until this point he had acted instinctively according to the plan which he had repeatedly rehearsed in his mind, but now his instincts also had become confused, failing to remind him that he should leave the room at once, go upstairs and get into bed. Several times he started slightly, feeling urged by a childish curiosity to turn the corpse over on its back so that he could see its face, but even this suggestion was so vague that he only became actively aware of it when his groping consciousness realized that the plunged dagger, protruding from the back, was in the way of such an act.

Immediately he uttered an exclamation of disgust and held out his two hands towards the hilt of the dagger. Blood had begun to ooze through the kimono all around the hilt. The blue silk had become a heavy, dark colour and one of the white stars had almost entirely disappeared.

'It will get ruined,' he said in a whisper.

He looked around the room furtively and then stooped over the corpse. He seized the dagger with both hands and tugged. The weapon had a curved blade and it had become firmly set in position by the stiffening of the body, so that it resisted all his efforts. That made him very excited and terrified, especially as blood now began to ooze freely from the wound and the corpse shifted to and fro as he pulled. He wanted terribly to let go his hold, to scream and run away and yet he kept pulling, until at last, he began to gibber hysterically. Then he became savage. He put his right foot on the corpse, bent down and made a final effort. The dagger rushed out, followed by a great spurt of frothing blood. With his foot still on the corpse, he gaped, uncomprehending, at this blood. Then he became horrified when he saw that it was staining his slipper. He dropped the dagger to the floor, drew back his foot and picked up the skirt of the kimono, to wipe the blood from his slipper. When he had done so, he dropped the skirt and then flushed with shame, seeing that the dead woman's naked thigh was exposed. With his face turned away, lest he might look again upon her nakedness, he drew the skirt gently down as far as it would reach. Then he stepped back, folded his arms on his bosom and said aloud:

'I must go upstairs now. It's getting late.'

He nodded assent to this statement several times, yet he could not persuade himself to move towards the door. Something which he could not understand held him in the room near the corpse. He felt vaguely that he had lost something precious, that he must find it and take it with him from the room.

At last he remembered that he had seen a photograph on the dressing table two months previously, on the night he had found the dead woman drunk in the bathroom and had put her to bed. He had also on that night been unwilling to leave the room, for some reason he could not understand. He had walked about after the woman had fallen into a stupor and gazed at the photograph; whereupon the woman had opened her eyes and said to him that the likeness had been made while she was 'still a silly young bitch.' For two months, while he contemplated the crime, the difference between the two faces, that of the woman and that of the girl in the photograph, had been an important factor in helping him to come to a decision.

Now he looked towards the dressing table, saw the photograph and decided to take it with him. He walked over slowly and looked at it. It was the size of a post card, set in a square, black, pasteboard frame. The picture was of the head and bust of a young girl, with long, golden hair and a countenance of great beauty and innocence. The medal worn by a Child of Mary hung around her neck. He picked up the photograph, sighed and put it in the pocket of his dressing gown. Then, without looking at the corpse, he walked casually to the door, turned the key and passed out into the hall, leaving the door wide open. He seemed quite calm and utterly indifferent as to what he had done; but when he had gone half-way up the first flight of stairs, he suddenly leaned against the banister, taken with a weakness that almost made him fall. Then he continued to ascend, with extreme caution, so weak that he could hardly move his feet. It took him almost a quarter of an hour to get to his garret. He listened outside his door and heard the sound of snoring from his neighbour's room. Immediately his weakness left him, and he realized that the cause of his anxiety had been that his neighbour might have left his room for some reason and seen the other door open (Ferriter had left it open through an oversight when he was going down). Now of course there was no danger of that, as the man had obviously been asleep all the time. He entered his room and locked the door.

It was now after three o'clock and dawn was breaking. He pulled up the blind and looked out. There was a great red blotch on the sky. He uttered a moan and covered his face with his hands. Then he staggered to the chair before his writing desk and sat down, still with his hands before his face. Yet he could not keep from his eyes the reflected vision of the red scar he had seen in the sky. He began to breathe heavily, and he was falling asleep through exhaustion when he roused himself, opened his eyes wide and whispered:

'I must not fall asleep like this. I might die. I'm ill. I must see a doctor.'

He began to sob and kept repeating that the world was very cruel, that he would never have any success in life, nor enjoy robust health like other young men. Then he saw the manuscript lying under the paper-weight. He picked it up and said angrily, holding it at arm's length:

'This, too, is an illusion.'

But this statement terrified him. He got to his feet and said in awe:

'My God! What have I said? That would be too horrible. I would be just a common murderer. I must hide this. It must be true, or the tortures of hell would become a reality in a world without God. Oh! Terrifying emptiness! Where could I turn? I must keep firm hold of myself. I must hide this and sleep. It's only weariness.'

He smiled dreamily and repeated:

'It's just because I'm tired. That's all.'

He went over to his bed, pulled back the cover and hid the manuscript under the pillow. Then he threw off his dressing gown and lay down He closed his eyes and fell asleep almost at once. Immediately he began to dream that people were searching for the manuscript. They kept coming nearer, until their hands were reaching out for the pillow. Then he gasped and awoke, with perspiration streaming from his forehead. He had only been asleep a few seconds. He got out of bed, took the manuscript from under the pillow and went over to the wardrobe, where he put it in his wallet. He returned to bed and tried once more to fall asleep, but now all desire for sleep had left him. He kept worrying about the manuscript and wondering whether it would not be better to destroy it, by burning it, or by tearing it into little bits and flushing the bits down the sink in the passage. Finally he decided to burn it. Again he got out of bed and put on his dressing-gown. As he was walking towards the wardrobe, he put his hands in the pockets of the gown and found the gloves and the photo-graph. This discovery threw him into a new state of terror. Forgetting all about the manu-script, he decided to burn the photograph, but

30

when he went to the fireplace and struck a match, he changed his mind and decided to keep the photograph and simply burn the frame. He did so and then put the photograph in the wallet with the manuscript. He returned to bed and fell asleep peacefully.

CHAPTER II

AT nine o'clock in the morning he was awakened
by a loud knocking on his door. He sat up,
rubbed his eyes and called out:

'Who is that?'

'It's me, Mr. Ferriter,' came the voice of Mrs.
Kelly, the caretaker's wife. 'For God's sake
open the door and let me in.'

He started on hearing her voice, like a person
who suddenly remembers something shameful
that has long lain forgotten in the memory.
That terrible secret which the veil of sleep had
hidden now sprang before his eyes, like a red-
nosed jumping Jack, with an idiot's grin upon
its face. He shook himself and then fell back,
but only for a moment. Even as he fell he had
begun to muster courage for the struggle to
outwit the eyes and brains of those who would
try to learn his secret.

'Just a moment,' he cried.

Then he got out of bed, put on his dressing
gown and opened the door. Mrs. Kelly rushed
into the room.

'Oh! Mr. Ferriter,' she cried at once, holding

out her clasped hands towards him. 'Something terrible has happened. Teresa Burke has been murdered. For God's sake don't tell anything about me to the police.'

She was a short, stout woman, with curly black hair, black eyes and a greasy, fat face, in which two qualities that rarely go together, greed and good nature, struggled for mastery to show their presence. For nearly a year now she had cleaned Ferriter's room every morning, and during this time she had always been exceedingly industrious, polite and obliging, yet he disliked her intensely. When he came to the house at first, the woman pitied him, because he was so thin and looked so sad. Out of her good nature, she used to bring him food and darn his socks and do his laundry; in fact she treated him as a son. Yet these solicitudes merely aggravated Ferriter's sensitive nature, for they reminded him of his poverty. He became harsh with her until she stopped doing him favours. Lately his dislike increased, when he discovered that she connived with the woman he had murdered to use the house as a brothel.

'Who is Teresa Burke?' he said slowly.

He spoke indistinctly, slurring his words, as his shark-like jaws injured his enunciation.

33

'God forgive me,' said Mrs. Kelly. 'What have I said? I mean Mrs. Boulter. She's been murdered, sir. Stabbed to the heart with a dagger. The police are in the house these two hours. I'm ruined if anything comes out.'

'Stabbed to the heart, did you say?' said Ferriter dreamily.

'Yes, sir,' she said, her black eyes roving over his face. 'For God's sake don't say anything to the police about me.'

'I expected this to happen,' said Ferriter in the same dreamy tone.

'I wanted to have a word with you beforehand,' she continued, 'so I ran up as soon as I could get a chance. They're questioning everybody in the house.'

Ferriter closed the door, folded his arms on his bosom and said to her in a haughty tone, like a judge passing sentence on a criminal:

'This woman about whom I complained has been killed, and you ask me to keep silent when questioned by the police. You want me to hide the fact that you allowed her to turn this house into a brothel. I look upon this murder as an act of divine vengeance, and I shall do everything in my power to expose everybody that has been responsible for it.'

34

Then he opened the door and motioned her to leave the room. She looked at him in amazement at first, as if she could not understand what he said. Then she cried out:

'You sneaking spy, you've been nosing around here since you came, but maybe your own soul is blacker than mine in spite of your holiness. I pitied you when you came into this house, but like a cur you turn on those that are kind to you. Do your best then. Do your best, and may the curse o' God light on you.'

He went very pale but he did not answer her. What she had said angered him, but he was also pleased by the effect which the murder had on her. She was one of those whom he wished to punish by his act. So he kept silent, holding the door open and looking straight in front of him haughtily. Then there were heavy footsteps on the stairs and a gruff voice called out:

'What's all this row here?'

Mrs. Kelly uttered an exclamation and left the room at once. Ferriter looked out and saw a Civic Guard come stooping up the narrow stairs.

'What are you doing here?' said the Guard to Mrs. Kelly.

'I just came up to call Mr. Ferriter,' she said.

The Guard looked up and saw Ferriter. Without moving out of the woman's way he said:

'Are you Mr. Ferriter?'

Ferriter nodded. The Guard pushed his way roughly past the woman, saying as he did so:

'Get downstairs you, and keep quiet, or I'll put a muzzle on you.'

'You better mend your manners or I'll report you,' she said.

'Go on now, you old rip.'

He followed Ferriter into the room, stooping to avoid the roof. He was very tall and slim, with a huge chest and very narrow hips. He looked enormous beside Ferriter, even though the latter was five feet ten inches in height. He looked suspiciously all round the room. His face was long like that of a horse, red and coarse, with an ill-shaped mouth in which the teeth stood like a ragged wooden paling; but his little eyes were very shrewd.

'What was that woman shoutin' for?' he said. 'Lookin' for the rent or what?'

'She came up to say that Mrs. Boulter, the woman who occupies the hall flat, has been murdered,' said Ferriter.

'Was that the first you heard of it?'

'Yes, I just woke up.'

'Well! It's grand to be you. Ye weren't very pleased at being woke up, then, by the row ye made.'

'I didn't make any row,' said Ferriter indignantly.

He was irritated by the policeman's familiarity. He had an obsession that everybody who tried to be at all friendly was merely being insulting; an obsession which developed since his father's bankruptcy and death had lowered his social position.

'It was she kicked up a row,' he continued, 'when I refused something she asked of me in connection with this murder.'

'And what was that?' said the policeman, taking out his note-book.

'I prefer to tell that to the proper authority,' said Ferriter.

'Ye may tell it to me,' said the policeman, tapping his chest with a pencil. 'I'm the proper authority.'

'I doubt it,' said Ferriter in a disdainful voice.

The policeman became so angry at Ferriter's impudent tone and the prospect of being unable to obtain, personally, information that might be important, that he stood erect with a sudden

37

movement and so struck his head a violent blow against the ceiling. This made him still more angry. His face went crimson.

'Well! In any case, Mr. Ferriter,' he said in a menacing tone, 'I have orders to make a report on the movements of all the inhabitants of this house last night. So ye better begin to tell me all about yourself. Look sharp now. Your full name and occupation?'

Speaking in the same insolent manner, Ferriter described his actions on the previous night, from the time he left the newspaper offices until the moment he entered his room after borrowing a cigarette from Fitzgerald. The policeman wrote all this down in his notebook.

'Now,' he said angrily, when he had finished, 'ye can tell the rest to the superintendent. Put on yer clothes an' get downstairs.'

'Certainly,' said Ferriter, 'if you'll kindly leave my room.'

'Eh?' said the policeman. 'I think I'll have a look around first.'

'Do as you please,' said Ferriter coldly.

The policeman floundered around the room for a little while and then went out, muttering under his breath. Ferriter closed the door after him and then smiled. He felt very pleased with himself. He had not expected to feel so composed when confronted by the police. One of the things that had made him hesitate for some time before definitely deciding to kill the woman was a fear that he might break down after the event and make a mess of things. Yet here he was, more cool than he had ever been in ordinary life. In fact, he delayed longer than usual with his toilet, feeling that the occasion demanded he should look as well as possible.

It was only when he was leaving the room that he suffered a relapse into the mood of terror of the previous night. Every morning, owing to his straitened circumstances, he was in the habit of counting all the money he had in his possession and making a calculation of how much he could afford to spend during the day. Finding fifteen shillings in silver in his trousers pockets he was surprised, because he could not remember having changed a note on the previous evening; so he took out his wallet to see whether there were three notes or just two in it. When he opened the wallet he saw the photograph and the manuscript. He closed the wallet at once and stuffed it into his pocket. Then he began to tremble.

'It's no use,' he muttered, looking around the room wildly. 'I'm caught. They are sure to search me and find these things in my wallet. Shall I hide it here? No, no. They are sure to search the room while I'm downstairs. That policeman obviously suspected me. My God! Did somebody see me last night?'

At that moment there was a loud knocking at the door and as he looked around in terror, the door opened and a man named Callahan, another journalist on the staff of the *Morning Star*, dashed into the room. This was a tall, dark, young man with a moustache, wearing a black hat and grey flannel trousers that were much too wide for him.

'Excuse me butting in like this, Ferriter,' he cried, 'but I just slipped past the cop on the stairs. I came up to see if you have any dope on this murder. Hell! I've been trying to get up for the last hour.'

He wiped his forehead with a handkerchief.

'God!' he said. 'You should see me sprint up those stairs. Tell me quick, though. Do you know anything?'

'How do you mean?' said Ferriter. 'I've just heard about the murder.'

'Yes, but you live in the house. Who is this lassie, anyway? Do you know her? I've dug up all the usual muck. In fact, I managed to get a dekko at the body, but I'm afraid it's not much good for us, unless there is some startling development. The bloody thing was discovered at the wrong time of the day. The evening papers 'll have it. See here. This is all I've got. Body discovered at seven o'clock by a young lady called Norah Beamish on her way to Mass, saw the corpse through the open door. Janey! She must have got a fright. She ran screaming into the street. I talked to an old lassie that met her outside. But they're all so damn stupid. Still . . . the police were quickly on the job. They've done all their tape measure and finger-print work. The medico has been here and apparently all is ready for parking the body in the morgue. The coffin has arrived. Looks like a straight piece of work. Not much blooming use to us. Give us all the dope you have about her, as the damn cops 'll tell nothing.'

Ferriter had gradually been getting angry while Callahan was speaking; principally because of the levity with which Callahan treated the 'sacrifice of blood.' Furthermore, Callahan had always treated him in a contemptuous manner, because of his very decided views on religion. Being himself somewhat of a libertine and an agnostic on the subject of God, Callahan often had violent quarrels with Ferriter, whom he accused of being 'one of the crew that are trying to turn this country into a bloody monastery.' In fact, the two men had not spoken to one another since their last quarrel some weeks previously.

And now he has the cheek to come to me for information, thought Ferriter.

'As a matter of fact,' he said in an insolent tone, 'I know a great deal about the woman and about certain events that preceded the murder, but I'm going directly to the editor with it. In any case, I dislike the vulgar manner in which you treat a very serious question like this.'

'Oh! You do, do you?' said Callahan, pushing his hat to the back of his head and putting his hand on his hip. 'Listen, Ferriter, old cock, I think you're a proper old . . .'

He used several foul expressions that made Ferriter livid with shame and rage. The two men would probably have come to blows had not the Civic Guard called out on the stairs at that moment, saying to Ferriter that the superintendent was waiting for him down below. Callahan, after threatening to see Ferriter later, strode out of the room.

'How in the name o' God did you get here, Mr. Callahan?' cried the Guard.

'I flew in through the roof,' said Callahan. 'Didn't ye know I had wings?'

'Well! Fly out the same way ye came in,' said the Guard. 'Ye're more trouble than ye're worth.'

'Same to you, sergeant.'

They all went downstairs. The whole house was in a state of violent excitement. Lodgers kept running in and out of their rooms asking questions of one another and relating as important every trivial incident they could remember that had any possible bearing on their association with the dead woman. There was an atmosphere of horror and at the same time, co-existent with this horror and feeding on it, the intense pleasure derived from the crime of murder by the mass of humanity.

Ferriter was conducted into the room where he had found the dagger.

CHAPTER III

As soon as he entered, he glanced towards the
mantelpiece, where the dagger had been hanging
in a sheath. The sheath was still there. At the
same time, he heard curious noises coming from
the bedroom, where he had committed the
murder. The noises were dulled by the closed
door and the curtain, but he suspected from what
Callahan had said that they were putting the
corpse into a coffin. For a moment he hesitated
and swerved, like a horse that has no courage
when called on for its effort in the finish of a race.
Then he turned his eyes swiftly to the right and
saw the eyes of three men watching him intently.
He immediately regained control of himself and
went forward steadily towards them. He did
not know that his face had lost all trace of
colour or that he was trembling, until one of the
men came forward and took him by the arm, as
if afraid that he was about to faint.

He brusquely pulled away his arm, looked at
the man indignantly and said:

'I beg your pardon.'

'Do you feel ill?' said another of the men,

sitting in an armchair by the window. 'Please sit down.'

'I've been ill recently,' said Ferriter in a low voice, 'and I've been rather upset by this . . . this business.'

'Take a chair, please,' said the man. 'You're Mr. Ferriter, aren't you? A journalist. You should be quite used to affairs like this.'

Ferriter sat down facing the man in the armchair.

'I'm not long a journalist,' he said quietly. 'In any case I only do social work. I've never done a murder case.'

'I see,' said the man, tapping the tips of his fingers together, with his thumbs against his chin and his arms on the elbows of his chair.

This man was Chief Superintendent John Lavan, who at the age of thirty-three had risen almost to the top of his profession, principally by virtue of that energy and ambition which is typical of public officials in this generation since the establishment of the Free State. This is particularly characteristic of the national police force, whose mechanism has been radically changed, so that together with being one of the most efficient police organizations in the world, it has also become an important factor in the

45

social life of the country. Lavan was a man of considerable information and culture, entirely devoid of that heavy and brutal manner which has come to be regarded as the classical attribute of a police officer. Dressed neatly in a double-breasted, blue serge suit, light of build and brisk of movement, with rosy cheeks and remarkably blue eyes, he looked like a smart, French army officer, more interested in glory and love affairs than in the detection and prevention of crime.

He remained silent for some time, examining Ferriter closely. The latter sat on the edge of his chair, leaning forward, his feet apart and his knees together, the palms of his hands joined between his thighs, like a monk disguised as a civilian. His rough tweed suit hung about his body like rags on a scarecrow. With his pale, hollow face and his eyes concealed behind his drooping lashes, he appeared to be absorbed in the contemplation of God, behind the circular rampart of his shark-like jaws. Indeed his face and his whole demeanour would have given him a fine dignity were it not for the ludicrous hat that lay perched on his head. It was made of grey tweed like his suit. But he had arranged it like a double-edged saucer, with the brim

46

turned up very close to the crown and the crown itself hollowed all around the edges in the American fashion, giving him the appearance of those music-hall comedians who arouse laughter by their melancholy buffoonery. In this case, however, the incongruity of dress did not arouse laughter but a suspicion that the man's brain was disordered.

'Now that I come to think of it,' said the superintendent, when he had finished his examination, 'I remember hearing something about you some time ago.'

Ferriter raised his head quickly and looked Lavan in the eyes.

'Really?' he said. 'This is a clever fellow,' he said to himself. 'I must beware of him.'

The superintendent smiled, took out a cigarette case and offered a cigarette to Ferriter. Ferriter shook his head.

'Don't you smoke?'

'Very rarely.'

'So? I wish I didn't. It's a dreadful habit. Yes. I remember something about you. That's correct. Ah! I have it. Don't you remember raiding a bookshop on the quays about two years ago?'

Ferriter started, but said nothing.

'Oh! There's nothing for you to worry about,'

said Lavan, tapping the end of his cigarette against his case. 'I merely mentioned the fact because your name reminded me of it. The bookseller begged us not to take any action, but we made enquiries all the same. I suppose he thought he was lucky to escape with having some of his property burned. However, these affairs were becoming too frequent at the time, and we went to the trouble of finding out the identity of the people who were implicated. You were one of them. That's how I remember your name. You were a law student at that time, as far as I can remember. So?'

'I'm not ashamed to admit that I was concerned in it,' said Ferriter with great dignity. 'The books we burned were immoral and a danger to the community. I was acting under orders in any case.'

'So?' said Lavan. 'I have no doubt they were immoral. No doubt at all. And you were acting under orders as you say. That's so. You were a member of a vigilance society. Quite true. It was recognized by leading members of the Church and by a number of prominent citizens. That's correct. No doubt there was even a considerable amount of popular feeling behind these acts. However, from the point of view of the police, these were acts of mob violence and illegal.'

Although he suspected that the superintendent had some ulterior motive in raising this matter, Ferriter could not prevent himself saying:

'You will admit that these acts achieved their purpose?'

'In what way?'

'The Censorship Bill would never have become law were it not for the moral courage of the young men who showed the government that they were determined to protect the community from corruption by the printed filth that was being sold.'

The superintendent quenched the match with which he had lit his cigarette and then threw it carefully into the fireplace.

'This is an interesting point of view,' he said. 'But I'm speaking as a police officer. My business is to enforce the law. My personal opinions are another matter. That's correct. I also am opposed to immoral literature. Quite true. You raise an interesting point, however, when you maintain that private citizens are justified in taking the law into their own hands in order to . . .'

'One moment,' said Ferriter excitedly. 'That's quite untrue.'

Now he felt sure that the superintendent was trying to trap him. He looked suspiciously at the burly detective-sergeant who was making notes at a little table near the fireplace. The sergeant stopped writing and began to tap his teeth with the end of his pencil.

'How do you mean?' said Lavan. 'You said just now . . .'

'I was referring to a very special case,' said Ferriter. 'You know very well that the whole country was roused on the subject of immoral literature. You are trying to generalize, though, from a particular case. I don't want you to think that I am of opinion that anybody is justified in taking the law into his own hands in order to rid society of some evil or other.'

'I see,' said Lavan calmly. 'I'm glad we agree on that point in any case. But now that we are on the subject, I think you will admit that these vigilance societies, acting on the best motives, might lead people into activities altogether, you might say, criminal and more dangerous than the activities they try to suppress.'

Now the superintendent seemed to become heated himself and Ferriter's suspicions were allayed, as he came to the conclusion that Lavan was really not as clever as he thought, and that he was merely a garrulous man giving air to his opinions; a habit common with policemen, who have a craze for using obscure language and toying with abstruse problems which they only vaguely understand, in order to pose as learned people.

'Excuse me,' he said rather insolently, 'but I can't see how you arrive at that conclusion.'

'How do you mean?' said Lavan.

'That membership of vigilance societies might lead people into criminal activities.'

'So?'

'Every sort of person is not allowed membership.'

'You think so?'

'I know it. Only persons of the highest moral character are admitted.'

'That may be so. But people of the highest moral character might be led astray through excess of zeal.'

'What do you mean by "led astray"?'

'Into breaking the law.'

'The law is not something fundamental and unchangeable. It is continually in need of reformation at various points. It is only sacred when it's in keeping with the highest interests of the community.'

'So? That is a very strange theory.'

'It's not at all strange. Nearly all reforms are brought about by a breach of existing laws. If I might use an example, you owe your rank to a revolution, which owed its success to armed revolt and murder, judging it from the point of view of the government that was overthrown.'

He said this in a very pointed and insolent manner, obviously wishing to convey that the chief superintendent himself had once been a revolutionary, branded as an outlaw by the British Government. But Lavan was not moved in the slightest.

'Don't think that I'm trying to persuade you that you are acting against the law,' he said, 'by being a member of your society.'

'Have I said that I am at present a member?' said Ferriter.

'Are you not?'

'No. I have resigned.'

'Why?'

'Pardon me,' said Ferriter in a superior manner, 'but I'd like to know whether I'm being examined officially in this matter.'

'Not at all,' said Lavan. 'I asked the question merely out of personal curiosity.'

At that moment there was a sound of hammering from the next room, and Ferriter started.

Lavan saw this movement and his eyes narrowed. But Ferriter looked him boldly in the eyes and said:

'That question really has some bearing on this unfortunate event, so I'll answer it.'

'Eh?' said Lavan. 'You mean on this murder.'

'Yes. It would not have happened if they had acted on my complaint.'

He became excited as he realized how really true this statement was and his head shook with emotion as he continued:

'I left the society two months ago because they refused to take action on a complaint I made to the committee, simply because one of the persons about whom I complained was the son of the most important member of the society.'

'Who was that?'

'Dr. Michael O'Leary.'

'The son of Mr. O'Leary of Dun. . . .'

'Yes.'

There was silence for some time. The sergeant opened his mouth and looked at the superintendent, who shook his head several times and pursed his lips.

'So?' said Lavan. 'And what connections had this complaint with the murder?'

'The murdered woman was the other person

about whom I complained,' cried Ferriter. 'For this murder the inefficiency of the law and the cowardice of certain members of the society are responsible.'

Ferriter made this statement in a loud voice and with flashing eyes, as if he were making a speech to a large audience; but as soon as he had finished speaking he realized that he had spoken dangerously. In fact, both the superintendent and the sergeant could not conceal their astonishment. It was not so much what he said that troubled him, as the manner in which he had spoken. Yet he could not prevent the sudden violence of his tone and gesture, for it was occasioned by sounds of footsteps and voices in the hall. They were carrying something to the door; the coffined corpse of the murdered woman. These sounds had horrified him and made him rebel against the necessity that had been imposed on him to make that sacrifice of blood. On hearing these sounds he realized how heavy a burden his secret was going to be, and what a great labour it would be to make society feel the significance of his act.

As Lavan was about to speak, somebody opened the door and called him. He arose and went out. The third man, who had tried to take

54

Ferriter by the arm and who had been standing all this time in a corner, now went to the window and peered out behind the curtains into the street. Ferriter examined him with great interest, feeling that his presence was unaccountable and strange, as he did not look like a policeman or fit company for respectable people. He was no more than five feet in height, very broad about the body, with a tiny head, which he kept moving to and fro continually, like a hen searching for food. His face had so little outward expression of character that it seemed to be devoid of features. Looking at him, Ferriter merely received a vague impression of a receding chin and a jutting upper lip. He wore a brown suit which had obviously been bought ready-made of a standard size as the coat was about six inches too long for him. A large watch-chain of imitation gold dangled across his stomach as he leaned forward to look out the window.

Ferriter was sure that he had seen this man before, yet he could not remember where. This disturbed him somewhat, but he felt reassured when the little man, on leaving the window, looked at him without recognition.

Then the superintendent returned and sat down hurriedly.

'Sorry to keep you waiting, Mr. Ferriter,' he said. 'You were saying. . . .'

'I'd like to make a clear statement about the whole matter,' said Ferriter.

'Very well. Go ahead.'

Ferriter cleared his throat and began to speak slowly.

'I came to live in this house a little over a year ago. About three months after I came these two rooms were rented by an Englishman named Boulter and his wife. They bought the furniture from a friend of mine, a journalist, who returned to Australia to take a job on a paper in Sydney. Soon, however, they became a nuisance and I dropped their acquaintance on discovering that they were not respectable people.'

'Then you knew them?'

'Not exactly socially. I began by having dealings with them about the furniture, which my friend asked me to sell for him. He had to go away suddenly before he could complete the bargain.'

'I see. In what way did they become a nuisance?'

'In many ways. They had drunken parties in their rooms, mostly attended by undesirable characters connected with racing and suspicious women. I believe Boulter himself had been a bookmaker or something of that sort in England. I know that he was mixed up while he was here with shady trafficking in Sweep tickets. He had left the house when I came out of the nursing home at the end of January, but his wife stayed on here. Then it became still more unpleasant, and I very soon realized that she was using these rooms for immoral purposes. I noticed different men coming and going at all hours of the day and night.'

'Then you complained to your society?'

'Not at that time. I complained to Mrs. Kelly, the caretaker's wife, who was aware, to my knowledge, that the rooms were used for immoral purposes.'

'How did you learn that? Did you just have a suspicion or did you get positive proof?'

'I had very definite proof.'

'So?'

Ferriter's face flushed a deep red and he said in a loud voice:

'One night when I was coming home from my office I heard sounds of a violent quarrel in Mrs. Boulter's rooms. I waited for a few moments on the stairs, wondering should I pay no attention or knock at her door and make a complaint about her conduct. It had by then become positively disgusting. Finally I turned back, knocked at the door and told them plainly what I thought of them. Then the door opened and Dr. O'Leary came out. He was drunk and used the most foul language to me, threatened me and pushed me back against the stairs. I went upstairs. Some time later, when I came down to the bathroom, I found Mrs. Boulter there, lying in a helpless condition on the floor. Apparently she had come up to wash blood from her face, as her lower lip was still bleeding when I found her, and there was a blood-stained towel lying on the floor beside her. She was so drunk that she couldn't stand. I helped her to her room and on the way she kept muttering that O'Leary had tried to murder her. She said something about having him in her power, and I gathered that O'Leary had been responsible for her ruin. She admitted frankly that she was a prostitute and acted in a most shameless manner.'

'Did she say how O'Leary was in her power?' said Lavan.

'Not definitely, but I gathered that she was blackmailing him at that time or at least threatening to do so.'

'You say she acted in a shameless manner.

Do you mean that she gave you the impression that she . . .'

'She convinced me,' cried Ferriter, in an exalted tone, 'that she was a soul abandoned by God. She was unclean.'

'You mean diseased?'

'Eh?' cried Ferriter, looking in wonder into Lavan's eyes. 'Is not sin the most foul disease?'

'That's correct,' said Lavan briskly. 'That's so. Then you were deeply affected by this incident and you decided to complain. So?'

'Naturally I didn't want to go on living under the same roof with a harlot. In the morning I complained to Mrs. Kelly, but she denied all knowledge of any irregularity, saying also that it was curious I was the only one of the tenants who complained. Yet I was constantly seeing the men that visited Mrs. Boulter coming in by the back entrance, through Mrs. Kelly's quarters in the basement. They went out the same way, and Mrs. Kelly ran errands to the public-house for them. But she denied it all.'

'That is very interesting,' said Lavan. 'What happened afterwards?'

'I then complained to the society, but they refused to take any action.'

'May I ask what action did you suggest they

should take and why you didn't complain to the police?'

Ferriter did not answer for some time. He knew that this was a dangerous question for him to answer and that he must choose his words carefully. At last he said:

'As the law stands at present, it's quite useless to complain to the police about cases like this. I hold very decided views about the evils of prostitution and consider that both parties to this immoral traffic are equally guilty, whereas in the eyes of the law only the woman is guilty. I consider that the man should be punished equally with the woman, as he has shared in the guilt.'

'So?' said Lavan. 'But in what way could your society punish them?'

'By public exposure for one thing, until such time as public opinion is sufficiently moved to demand a change in the law, making it a legal offence for a man to have dealings with a prostitute.'

'I see. And they refused to take action.'

'They refused for the reason I told you before, because the man I cited was the son of one of the committee.'

'And then you decided . . .'

Both men looked very closely at one another, as Lavan paused in his sentence. Then Ferriter said:

'I beg your pardon.'

'What did you decide to do then?' continued Lavan.

'I decided to let things take their course,' said Ferriter slowly. 'I came to the conclusion that these two damned souls were going headlong to their destruction and that I could do nothing to stop them; that a higher power had determined to wreak vengeance.'

Lavan looked at him with astonishment.

'I don't altogether understand you,' he said.

'It's not difficult to understand,' said Ferriter arrogantly, 'if you have faith as a Christian that God rules the destinies of human souls. Sodom and Gomorrah were destroyed.'

Lavan's face expressed increasing astonishment.

'Then you think this murder was an act of God,' he said.

'I am convinced of it,' said Ferriter calmly. 'In fact, for some time I KNEW that it would happen.'

At this moment, the sergeant dropped his pencil and said to himself:

'That man is mad.'

61

And Lavan, pursuing up his lips, asked himself:

'Is it this daft fellow or is it not?'

'You have made a very extraordinary statement,' he said aloud, in a severe tone. 'You say you knew this was going to happen. Then you must know the murderer.'

'Yes,' said Ferriter, looking him straight in the face. 'I know the murderer.'

Now even the tiny man, who had been standing idly in the background, listless and indifferent, had become visibly excited by what Ferriter had said and by the strange manner in which he had spoken. Indeed, the three men, habitually used to contact with violent sensation, with murder, treason and all the most grave sins against society, had been moved by the fanatic's manner and personality more than by the crime itself. There is inherent in our Irish nature a profound respect for those obscure regions of the human soul where mystic phantoms fill the void past reason's limits, so that among us the madness of 'holy' men has a somewhat sacred character, as if we understood their brains have grown sick with much labour, seeking the meaning of the all-important mystery.

Ferriter was pleased by the effect he had

produced. He felt like an actor on the stage, who even while carried away into a state of exaltation by the heroic part he is miming, still watches the audience through his own paltry senses, in order to enjoy his success.

'Well,' said Lavan after some time. 'Who is the murderer?'

Ferriter shrugged his shoulders.

'I can't tell you,' he said mournfully.

'What?' cried Lavan, sitting bolt upright in his armchair.

'I may be convinced as to the identity of the person responsible for the murder,' continued Ferriter calmly, 'but it is quite another thing to be able to make a definite accusation that would bring that man to the scaffold. In the same way that I was unable to persuade the society to take action that would prevent the murder, so am I now unable to persuade the law to take action that would bring this man to the gallows. You must find out yourselves. It is all in the hands of God.'

'He's a daft fool,' thought Lavan, sitting back disappointedly.

'Then you merely have suspicions,' he said aloud.

'Legally, that is so,' said Ferriter.

'On what do you base these suspicions?'

'That question is too general,' said Ferriter quietly. 'It would involve too many side issues, that are important in so far as my reasoning is concerned, but of no importance to you, who are merely concerned with the purely legal aspect of this crime.'

'He's not such a fool after all,' thought Lavan. 'When you said just now that this murder would not have happened if the society took the action you suggested,' he continued, 'did you mean to infer that O'Leary had killed Mrs. Boulter?'

Suddenly the exalted expression left Ferriter's countenance and he looked old, sick and exhausted. His cheeks were as hollow and colourless as those of a corpse, above his heavy, shark-like jaws. In his eyes there was a look of pain. When the moment arrived to accuse O'Leary definitely as the murderer he could not get himself to do so; for as he understood it there were two men concerned in the murder, the one who had made the sacrifice of blood and the other who had murdered the woman's soul. Feeling that he was cornered, he took refuge in an outburst of anger.

'It would be foolish for me,' he cried, 'to bring the enmity of these important people down on my head by making any such suggestion to you.

I am a poor journalist, without money or friends, of no social importance whatsoever. Hadn't you better ask O'Leary himself where he spent his time from three o'clock yesterday afternoon, when he entered this house from the lane at the back and whether it was his voice I heard in Mrs. Boulter's room as I passed through the hall after midnight last night? Ask Mrs. Kelly whether she brought drink into these rooms yesterday evening. She will be able to tell you whether O'Leary was there. She will also be able to tell you whether he has been a regular visitor to this house for the past two months, generally spending each week-end with Mrs. Boulter. It's not for me to make these suggestions. Already I am a persecuted man, because I value the service of God above that of Mammon.

'Then you saw O'Leary enter the house yesterday afternoon.'

'Yes. I saw him from my window.'

'Did you just happen to be at your window, or were you watching for him?'

'Why should I watch for him?'

'You just happened to be sitting at your window.'

'Yes. I was writing, and I sat at the window to get as much sunlight as possible.'

'I see. And last night when you were coming in you heard his voice.'

'I didn't say I heard his voice. I heard a man's voice in her room.'

The superintendent remained silent for a little while and then he asked several questions relative to Ferriter's movements since he entered the house on the previous night, explaining that it was a matter of routine. Then he took out a packet of cigarettes and again offered one to Ferriter. Again Ferriter refused.

'Oh! Of course you don't smoke, do you?' said Lavan.

'Very rarely,' said Ferriter.

'I see. Well! That will do for the present. Oh! One moment. I had almost forgotten to ask you whether you heard any sounds of any sort or noticed anybody when you came down to the bathroom last night.'

He had said this in a very casual way, but Ferriter started violently.

'How do you mean?' he said in a thick voice.

Lavan looked at him sharply for a few moments and then smiled.

'Oh! Of course it wasn't last night you found her in the bathroom.'

'No,' said Ferriter almost in a whisper.

66

'You went to bed after you borrowed the cigarette from Fitzgerald?'

'Yes,' whispered Ferriter. 'I went to bed.'

'Very well,' said Lavan, getting to his feet. 'That will do for the present. Thanks very much. You have given us very important information. I'll let you know if we want your evidence at the inquest.'

He nodded and Ferriter got to his feet. He was trembling and he licked his lips nervously. He was trying to say something further, but he could not remember what it was and his tongue could not articulate the words. So he turned about and walked slowly out of the room. The three men followed him with their eyes. When the door had closed behind him, the superintendent beckoned the tiny man.'

'Tyson,' he said, 'get after that fellow and keep an eye on him. Don't lose him on any account, and report to me anything suspicious.'

The little man slouched noiselessly out of the room. Lavan looked at the floor for a long time and then rubbed the palms of his hands together briskly.

'Well! Sergeant,' he said. 'This is an interesting case. Very funny young man, that Ferriter. He doesn't smoke, or hardly ever smokes and yet he knocks a man up at one o'clock in the morning to borrow a cigarette. That fool O'Leary seems to be in for a stomach full of trouble in any case. I want Mrs. Kelly down at headquarters. She'll probably talk now. Come along.'

CHAPTER IV

WHEN Ferriter emerged into the street, he found the pavement blocked by a crowd of people, whom two policemen were trying in vain to disperse. The identity and profession of the murdered woman had already become known in the neighbourhood. The crowd, being mainly composed of slum dwellers, was exceedingly violent against the murderer. They were of opinion that an injury had been done to one of their class by some rich person. The departure of the coffined body had particularly agitated them. Two women were shaking their fists at the police and saying that there was one law for the rich and another for the poor. It must be understood that the economic condition of that district had suffered considerably since the closing of the brothel quarter by the government after the revolution. For this reason, the crowd associated the police with the murder. Among the poor, the police are never regarded as the upholders of the common law, but as agents of the rich to oppress those without property.

At first, Ferriter was unable to understand the cause of the uproar; but when he realized that the people were sympathetic with the murdered woman he grew angry. For the first time since he had plunged the dagger he felt exalted by what he had done. His eyes blazed with a fanatical hatred of the ragged people, whom he regarded as living symbols of that sin which his sacrifice of blood would destroy on earth. His blood became triumphant in his veins and he saw that other blood as poison issued from a snake, which had been struck down in God's name.

With his hands in the pockets of his shabby coat, he walked disdainfully through the crowd, quite prepared to have them spit on him, rend his clothes, stone him, shout curses in his ears. But when they took no notice of him whatsoever and he passed into Beresford Place, where life was proceeding calmly, as if no murder had been done, his exaltation vanished, having no anger upon which to feed. In its place came a sense of desolation, so intense that it was physical, rising in a grey cloud from the earth and pressing on him at all sides. There was a sultry heat and the sky was heavy with signs of coming thunder. The air stood still, so that the tumult of the city's traffic sounded as in a vast, gloomy hollow, where life has no purpose, all grey and forbidding. Then he had the hallucination that he was walking alone in this gloomy valley, dripping with blood, while a crowd of people afar off raised their arms and cried out in condemnation. He walked without end and the blood kept pouring from him, until the valley was flooded with it. And he heard a voice cry out:

'I am the lamb of God, who washeth away the sins of the world.'

The vision disappeared as he heard this voice, and his reason asked:

'Can the world be washed clean of sin in the blood of a harlot, who is a symbol of impurity? Has my soul become stained by this impure blood, and am I then a murderer?'

Now a veil was torn from his mind and he saw how he had moved, as in possession of an alien spirit, from the moment he had conceived the killing on the stairs, until just now when he had seen his image wandering in the valley of blood. He halted suddenly, as he was turning the corner into Middle Abbey Street.

'Oh! My God!' he said half aloud.

He was horrified at the thought that the person who had planned and executed the murder was somebody different from himself, a spirit who had used his body to fulfil a purpose and had now vanished, leaving a sense of desolation.

'Must I always suffer like this?' he cried aloud. 'Oh! God! This is too cruel. I can't endure it. Have pity on me.'

He walked on hurriedly towards O'Connell Street. At the intersection of Marlboro' Street, he looked towards the left to see if any traffic were coming from the quays before he crossed the road. He noticed the tiny man reading a notice board outside the pit entrance to the Abbey Theatre. He started. At once he dashed across the road in front of a motor lorry, which tooted its horn loudly and swerved in order to avoid him. When he reached the far pavement, he glanced back at the tiny man. The fellow was still examining the notice board.

'It's ridiculous,' he said as he walked on. 'He's not following me. He merely chanced to be walking along the same way. My God! I should definitely have denounced O'Leary as the murderer and Mrs. Kelly, too. Did I not take special note of the way she carried her overcoat loose over her shoulders when she was bringing in the bottles? They can't suspect me. Impossible.'

Yet, when he looked back again at the corner

of O'Connell Street and saw the little man coming along the street on the far side, he became still more anxious. He crossed the mouth of Middle Abbey Street, glanced at the tiny man who was now quite close and then walked quickly down O'Connell Street for a few yards to an Italian café which he entered. He waited inside the door at a fruit counter. After a few moments he saw the little man pass the doorway. The man nodded slightly as he passed. At least he seemed to have done so, but his personality was so vague that it was hard to say whether he nodded or not. In any case, Ferriter felt relieved. He sighed and went to the rear of the café to have some breakfast. Having ordered a dish of bacon and eggs, with tea and rolls, he placed his head between his hands and said to himself:

'Now I must not allow myself to become hysterical. That's all it amounts to, when one begins to have doubts and visions of an unpleasant sort. I must prevent myself having any doubts about the justice of what I have done, otherwise I shan't be able to go through with the rest of my programme. I must put the neck of the sensualist in the noose.'

He shuddered as he visualized a body dangling in a noose. His own body? He got to his feet hurriedly and went downstairs into the lavatory. He locked himself in a cabinet and took the manuscript and the photograph from his wallet, intending to tear them up into small pieces, drop them in the basin and pull the chain. But the sight of the basin caused such revulsion in him that he could not do so. He was putting them back into his wallet when he reflected that if he were searched, they would certainly look in his wallet. He might even drop either one or the other by chance on taking out his wallet to produce his card in the course of his work. He decided to hide them inside his socks. He put the manuscript inside his left sock and the photograph inside his right sock. This calmed his fears and he ate a hearty breakfast, reviewing in his mind, while he ate, the plan he intended placing before the editor of the *Morning Star*.

He left the café and crossed the street towards the office, still so immersed in his plan that he did not trouble to see whether the tiny man was still following him. Yet the fellow was close on his heels when he entered the door of the newspaper building.

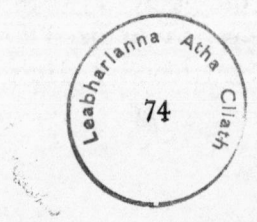

CHAPTER V

'THEY'RE reeking with filth,' cried Mr. Patrick
Corish, editor of the *Morning Star*, as he shook his
fat fists at copies of two London rival newspapers
that he had spread on the table of his private
office beside his own paper. 'Dirty cross-Channel
rags, without God or country, or sense of decency
either. They're at it again, the bloody English,
creeping in by the sewers, after we had them
driven out on the field of battle.'

Mr. Corish was a very stout man of fifty-five,
with short legs, a florid face and heavy pouches
under the eyes. All the top of his head was bald,
but there was a thick mane of grizzly, whitish
hair at the back of his neck. An excellent family
man and extremely kind in his personal relation-
ships, he was utterly devoid of character or prin-
ciple in his profession; and it was this weakness
to which he owed his success in journalism, added
to a fine frenzy of words and a knack for understanding the more base instincts of the mass of
humanity. Now, however, he and his newspaper
had come to a crisis in their joint career.

To use the language of journalism, the *Morning Star* was 'a national organ of popular opinion.' In reality, it was the property of a powerful group of Dublin business men, representative of that Catholic middle class that has risen to prosperity with the collapse of the landowning class and the change from feudalism to democracy. During the armed struggle waged by this Catholic middle class against the British Government from 1918 to 1921 and again during the civil war, waged in the two succeeding years by the new middle-class rulers (who had deposed their old masters) against the poorer peasants and labourers that wished to share the spoils of victory, the *Morning Star* had increased its circulation enormously. Although neither the proprietors nor the editor were nationalist or revolutionary, being solely concerned with making money, during that period of general excitement they equalled the most fanatical in patriotic violence. In private, however, they protected themselves from arrest or hanging by lavishly entertaining British officers and officials, whom they advised the people to kill in their newspaper. Mr. Corish, especially, was noted for his private hospitality to the 'armed hirelings of the national enemy,' as he called British officers in print; and in that way he managed very well to run with the hare and hunt with the hounds. He became an important person, a real power in the country. The coffers of his proprietors were bursting with dividends.

Then the Free State Government began to set the affairs of the country in order, ensuring peace and stability by rigid measures, without however introducing that Utopia for the wretched common people which had been promised by the Catholic middle class in its struggle for power. The people began to grumble and to call the *Morning Star* 'a dirty rag.' Therefore the *Morning Star* had to find a new god for the people to worship. When Dr. Johnson said that patriotism was the last refuge of a scoundrel he could not have meant his words to apply to Ireland; for in our country that last refuge is religion. Mr. Corish and the proprietors of his newspaper fell back on religion in an attempt to retain their circulation and to prevent the masses from buying the English newspapers that began again to become popular. They joined hands with the Catholic clergy, who were then starting their great campaign to consolidate their power under the new government by completely destroying the remnants of the old Protestant middle class. The *Morning*

Star became the official organ of the new Puritanism which began to sweep the country.

For a time this campaign promised to be successful for Mr. Corish, as people really believed in the menace of Freemasonry and in the conspiracies hatched against the Catholic Irish people by the Protestant hierarchy, Dublin University and the rich Protestant business people of Dublin. The Censorship Act was passed, intending to prohibit all publications considered immoral by the Catholic Church. But the cunning English newspapers found a means of circumventing this law, by printing Irish editions, which omitted all matter that might give offence to the Catholic Church Puritans. The unfortunate Mr. Corish found himself in a worse position than before. Now the enemy was at his very gates, with branch offices in Dublin and sales managers touting all over the country. And the god of Puritanism which he had called to his assistance now had him in chains, preventing him from fighting his enemy with any chance of success. His paper was being turned into the official organ of the Irish Catholic hierarchy, its principal news page covered with the photographs of cardinals, bishops and nuns, its leading articles pious sermons, hardly daring to mention Ireland or Irish affairs lest he might give offence to some village priest or fanatic. Nor was he able to print violence against the English as in the old days, for now his principal advertisers were English capitalists who had opened factories in Dublin, following the import duties imposed by the Free State government to encourage Irish industries.

He began to pace up and down the floor, with his hands clasped behind his back, halting now and again at the table to shake his fists at his English rivals, whose news was admittedly much more interesting than his own, since it was concerned less with the affairs of the next world than with this. The proprietors were grumbling. Dividends were falling. His importance as a public man had dwindled almost to vanishing point. The magnificent new building in which the paper was housed, raised on the profits of the boom years, no longer attracted admiring American capitalists to its roof, nor did Mr. Corish's photograph appear in local American newspapers as 'the big boy of the Irish news world.' In fact, Mr. Corish saw nothing but ruin staring him in the face.

'God Almighty!' he cried. 'I don't know where to turn. Here are these blasted rags, gone to press yesterday evening and brought over here from Holyhead on last night's mail boat, pretending to have to-day's news. It's awful. And they get away with it.'

A boy entered to say that Mr. Ferriter wanted an interview. At first Mr. Corish cursed the boy, but he changed his mind and decided to see Ferriter, whom he disliked and on whom he wished to vent his displeasure at that moment.

'He's another of these half-wits that have been foisted on me,' he said to himself bitterly. 'I'll give him a piece of my mind.'

Of late he was forced to take on his staff melancholy young men whose sole qualification for journalism was membership of some Catholic organization, or relationship with an important citizen. Ferriter had been recommended by an aunt, who was the wife of a Cabinet Minister and one of the leading hostesses under the new regime.

'One of these days,' thought Mr. Corish, as he saw the pale face and limp body of Ferriter enter the room, 'I'm going to murder one of these fellahs. Then I'll throw myself in the river. Well, young man!' he said aloud, 'what have you got to say? Speak up. Why don't you pull yourself together and look lively? They tell me you live in the house where that woman was murdered last night. This is a nice hour of the day for you to turn up here and the dogs of the city yelping the news already. Do you know it was your business to rush over to the . . .'

'Excuse me, sir . . .' began Ferriter.

'Bosh!' shouted Mr. Corish. 'Excuse your grandmother. You're a very disappointing young man. I took you on here out of respect for your aunt, but what have you done since you came here? What have you done, I say? Speak up, damn it.'

'But I want to say . . .'

'Speak up then, and tell me what you want to say. I'm asking you what you have to say.'

Thereupon Mr. Corish turned his back on Ferriter and began to pace the room with his hands behind his back, muttering to himself about 'a blooming gang of craw-thumpers, louts and lunatics.'

'He is a vulgar and a coarse man,' said Ferriter to himself, looking at the editor's fat legs from under his lowered eyelids.

'Well!' said Mr. Corish, halting at the end of the room and looking fiercely at the young man. 'I'm waiting for you.'

Ferriter sniffed, drew up his left shoulder and said in a low voice:

'I wish to say that I have very important information about the death of Mrs. Boulter.'

'You mean the woman that was murdered?'

'Yes.'

'Ha! Out with it then.'

Ferriter repeated what he had said to the superintendent. When he had finished, he found to his astonishment that Mr. Corish seemed aghast instead of being pleased.

The editor remained silent for some time and then he said:

'Good God! Tim O'Leary's son. It's incredible.'

Mr. Tim O'Leary was a prominent citizen, a personal friend of Mr. Corish and a leading member of many religious organizations. Mr. Corish, therefore, realized that it would do the *Morning Star* no good to expose the connection of Mr. O'Leary's son with the murder. So he turned angrily on Ferriter and said:

'You're out of your mind, young man.'

'I beg your pardon,' said Ferriter.

'Keep your mouth shut about this.'

'I don't understand you, sir,' said Ferriter.

'In the name of God,' shouted Mr. Corish, 'are you a total fool?'

Ferriter became angry.

'Don't you realize this is a wonderful opportunity for the *Morning Star*,' he cried, 'to expose the immorality that is disgracing this city.'

'What's that you say?' cried Mr. Corish. 'Young man, did I or did I not hear you opening your mouth to tell me how this paper should be run and what should be printed in it? Am I out of my senses, or is it really true that in my old age things are come to this pass, when a cub like you can come into my office and give me advice? Ordering me, are you? Eh? Speak up. Do you dare come in here and give me advice?'

Fearing that he had excited himself too much and placed himself in danger of getting a stroke (his doctor had recently warned him), the editor again began to walk up and down, muttering to himself:

'I'm a fool to lose my temper with a young fellah like that.'

Ferriter was not at all defeated at this outburst. He had grown very pale, but his diffident nature had sucked arrogance from this assault on his dignity, as is the rule with such types. He had taken off his ridiculous hat and now his head looked noble, with his limp, fair hair hanging in a Napoleonic attitude over his right temple. Leaning on his left leg, with his right shoulder raised, he looked as passive as a sleeping horse, but his shark-like jaws, set firmly, showed his strong determination.

'I humbly apologise,' he said in a very insolent tone, 'if I gave you the slightest impression that I was being impertinent. I have no intention of offering you advice, Mr. Corish, but I expect you as a fellow Catholic to take the correct stand on this matter and to spare nobody concerned in this affair, no matter what his social importance may be. I expect you also to recognize that you have a duty to God and to your country as editor of an important newspaper, which you should use as an instrument to root out the evil of sin.'

'What's that you're saying?' gasped Mr. Corish, inarticulate with rage. 'Do — do — do you think the *Morning Star* is a penny pamphlet or — or — or the official organ of the Salvation Army? Do you want the whole world to think Dublin is overrun with brothels? Do you want to bring the Government and the Church down on top of me? It's bad enough as it is, with all the old hags in the country prying into everything I print, without . . . without . . . Great Scott!'

Mr. Corish got red at the gills, paused for a few moments, trying to think of something violently abusive, and as he could think of nothing, he yelled:

'Get out of here. You're sacked. Do you hear? Get out. You're sacked.'

On hearing these words, Ferriter's arrogance vanished in an instant. He was dumbfounded by this outcome of the interview, for he had expected nay, he had felt certain, that the editor would listen to his proposal and give him the task of writing the leading articles that would rouse the country to a holy war against immorality. Had he not seen himself as the leader of this holy war while the divine fire of fanaticism was preparing him to commit the murder? Was not the manuscript in his wallet a treatise on the divine right to conduct such a war? And instead of that he was being dismissed, left penniless.

And then he felt a recurrence of that brutality which exalted him at the moment he was plunging the dagger into the woman's back. Now he wanted to strike down in the same manner the man who stood before him. His face became so terrible that Mr. Corish drew back instinctively. But now there was no purpose behind this murderous inclination. Almost at its inception it produced a nausea of the stomach. He bowed his head, turned around and walked slowly from the room, bowed down by a sense of defeat and humiliation. Now his desperate action appeared futile, and a sense of his danger drove him into a panic. As he hurried down the stairs he decided to fly at once from the city.

But when he was leaving the building he chanced to glance across the street and saw the tiny man standing against a shop window. Immediately, he changed his mind and determined to go to Lavan and definitely accuse O'Leary of the murder.

CHAPTER VI

In the meantime, on his return to police headquarters, Lavan found Dr. O'Leary waiting to
speak to him. They shook hands in a friendly
manner as they were more than casually acquainted.

'I'd like to have a few words with you, Jack,'
said O'Leary.

Lavan nodded and led the way into his private
office, followed by O'Leary and the sergeant.

O'Leary was a powerfully built man, almost
squat, with great limbs, neck and chest. He was
carelessly dressed in a suit of blue serge that was
slightly baggy at the knees and expansive at the
waist owing to the man's increasing corpulence.
Yet he looked extremely handsome, because of
his strength and carriage. He walked with the
rolling gait of a sailor, one leg very hooked, and
his head thrust forward aggressively from his
powerful neck, like a male beast in quest of
plunder. His features were cast in the same large
mould as the rest of his body and the skin of his
face bore a tawny gloss. His countenance was

saved from being brutal by blue eyes that were extremely gentle and innocent.

He was thirty-four years of age, yet he had only recently qualified as a doctor, after having been thirteen years a medical student, with the exception of a short period when he had wandered about England, doing odd jobs as a labourer. Since his school days he had been the black sheep of the family. Manifestly intended by nature for a country life, taming the earth and animals, or an adventurer in waste places, in command of men belonging to his own type, his parents had insisted, with that snobbery characteristic of our middle classes, that he should become a doctor. Year after year, thousands of young men, who might become excellent farmers, mechanics and artisans, are lost to the country through this shabby zeal of publicans, grocers and drapers for turning their sons into doctors, priests, lawyers and civil servants, professions which are considered socially respectable. Thus we witness the phenomenon of members of the old aristocracy concerning themselves with the breeding of pigs, poultry, cattle and horses, with the development of industry and the culture of the arts, while our middle class, which has just escaped from the menial state bordering on serfdom, has a horror of anything associated with manual labour. O'Leary's father had come from farming stock of the poorer sort, but he had made a large fortune in Dublin as a draper and was now a leader in the new social life ushered in by the revolution. So he wished his sons to enter the reputable professions, and for this reason Michael was destined to be a doctor, although he had no brains or inclination for the business. Irritated by his father's choice and yet afraid to rebel, lest he might lose his share of the inheritance, his physical strength and energy found an outlet in debauchery of the most abandoned sort, so that he had become known, even in his student days, as a proper rowdy and libertine. Now that he had qualified he was less wild, but no more successful at his work; for times have changed, and it is no longer possible for stupid doctors to purchase government appointments through the influence of their relatives, since corruption of this sort has been made difficult by recent laws. During the eighteen months since his qualification, he had been locum tenens for such of his friends as held dispensary practices in the neighbourhood of the city.

When they reached Lavan's office O'Leary pointed to the sergeant and said:

'Listen, Jack. Couldn't I speak to you alone?'

'Is it about some private matter?'

'It's about this murder.'

'Well! In that case, I'm afraid it's impossible.'

'Now, look here, Jack. I swear to you by all that's holy I had nothing to do with it.'

Lavan shook his head and sat down at his desk.

'Oh! All right,' said O'Leary. 'Go ahead. Start the fireworks. Take it all down. This is the blooming end of me. I can see that.'

He slung his hat on to a chair and then plunged into another chair near Lavan's desk, folded his arms and began to sniff, which action made the top of his nose and his little fair moustache move from side to side.

'You needn't worry, doctor,' said Lavan, 'that any information you give us about this affair is not going to be strictly confidential, so you can be quite frank. That is, of course, unless . . .'

'Unless you find out I murdered her,' interrupted O'Leary. 'Jasus! That's where I'm in a hole unless you can find the bloke that did it. I left her at two o'clock this morning, I may as well tell ye. What d'ye make o' that, eh?'

'I see,' said Lavan. 'Then you decided to come here?'

'What d'ye mean?' said O'Leary excitedly, leaning forward in his chair. 'I declare to Christ, Jack, you think I did it. Now, honour bright, you have a suspicion in your mind that I'm a bloody murderer. I wouldn't think it of ye, though.'

'Now, don't be a fool,' said Lavan coldly. 'You should know me well enough to understand that my attitude towards this murder is entirely impersonal. Until I lay hands on the criminal, I must suspect everybody who could possibly have committed the murder. That's so. As far as I can see, you're in a nice mess, O'Leary. It's up to you to help as far as possible in getting yourself out of it. You can do that only by telling your story as clearly and as calmly as possible. It will do you no good to shout or lose your temper.'

O'Leary had become very agitated and he even looked menacing as he leaned forward, with his powerful hands hanging loose between his thighs. His eyes had become cruel, and his tanned face was flushed. In fact his appearance at that moment was definitely that of a man capable of murder.

'But the point is this,' he shouted. 'How am I going to prove I'm innocent? I met Jack

Callahan in O'Connell Street. It was he told me about the murder, so I came along here after a bit. He said you fellahs had no idea who has done it. I knew there was no chance of my being able to keep out of the lousy business, on account of that dirty rat Ferriter. He saw me several times going into the house, and I had a row with him there one night. I was going to smash his face for him.'

'Do you know Ferriter well?' asked Lavan.

'Too well I know him, without knowing him at all, if you know what I mean,' said O'Leary, wiping his face with a large silk handkerchief. 'I never did him an ounce of harm, but he's been on my track like a ferret for the past few months. As you may know, my old man is nutty on religion and he's mixed up with all these societies for putting down immorality. What the hell does Ferriter do but come up before this society and make a complaint about me, saying I was in the habit of visiting a prostitute. Jasus! I'll murder that fellah if I lay hands on him.'

Hereupon he jumped to his feet and looked about him wildly.

'Calm yourself, for goodness sake,' said Lavan. 'It's a good job for you that I know you or your conduct'd be most damning evidence against you.'

O'Leary looked about him vaguely, curled up his lips and then tumbled back into his chair.

'Oh! What the hell do I care?' he said. 'I'm fed up. Listen, Jack, d'ye mind if I have a drink?'

He took a baby bottle of whisky from his pocket.

'I bought a couple of babies on my way here,' he said as he pulled the cork, 'to give myself courage.'

He put the bottle to his head and emptied it. Then he laughed and wiped his mouth.

'Now pull yourself together,' said Lavan.

'Oh! I'm fed up to the teeth,' said O'Leary gloomily. 'After being all these years trying to qualify, this misfortune comes on top of me. See here, it's the work of all these cursed religious maniacs that are making life a misery in this city. If they had their way they'd prosecute a man for going to bed with his wife. Tell me, though. Callahan told me she was stabbed. Was it with that dagger that was hanging on the wall in the sitting-room? It was. Poor Tess! To think you'd end like that! I feel myself responsible for it. I declare to God I do.'

He drew his large hands slowly over his face. Then he looked pathetically at Lavan and said:

'Jack, I loved that girl. I should have married

her if I had any guts. I might be out in Canada or in the States, doing well. But I didn't have the courage to cut loose.'

'So?' said Lavan.

O'Leary again took out his handkerchief and blew his nose violently. Then he shook himself, drew in a deep breath and said almost in tears:

'She was one o' the best, a bit daft, but with a heart of gold, once you got to it.'

'So?' said Lavan. 'You knew her for some time then?'

'Eight years,' said O'Leary. 'I met her when I was attending St. John's Hospital. She was a nurse there. She had just come up from the country. She was only eighteen at that time, the finest looking girl you ever saw. I went clean daft about her. Can you blame me? Ye know the way a fellah goes on? We're all in the same boat as far as that is concerned. You know what I mean, Sergeant. I'm making no insinuations, Jack, but we're all the same, if the truth were known. All is fair in love and war.'

'Yes, yes,' said Lavan irritably. 'Carry on with your story.'

'I'll háve another drink first,' said O'Leary. 'Jasus! I could cry if I were a woman. I feel myself responsible for everything.'

He emptied another baby bottle. Then he remained motionless for some seconds with his head dangling. Then he spat with great force into his handkerchief.

'I've no brains, Jack,' he cried in an angry voice. 'That's the trouble with me. When anything goes wrong, I just lash out and lose my head. Ye see, Tess got in the family way, and I could do nothing for her, so I went to the old man and told him all about it, saying I wanted to marry her and to give me enough money to go to Canada. God! He got wild, so I broke up the house and cleared over to England. I didn't mean to leave Tess in the lurch. In any case, they gave her some money — at least my mother did — and she went home to her place at first. I meant to send for her when I got some money together in England. God! I don't know now exactly what happened. I'm all mixed up. Send one of the lads out for another drink.'

'No,' said Lavan. 'You've had enough to drink. This is no time to get drunk, man alive.'

In fact, O'Leary was already slightly drunk. Although he was an habitual drinker, the two measures of whisky had gone to his head owing to his excitement.

95

'That's a fact,' he said. 'There's no use getting tight. I'd have to keep tight all my life to forget this. Although, I declare to God I meant to do the right thing by her, but when I got to England, what with one thing an' another, I got mixed up with a gang of workmen: they have a different way of looking at things. It was the happiest time of my life, frying steaks off shovels and drinking pints in four-ale bars. I wrote her a couple of letters, but I could never save any money, an' she didn't come over. The letters were the cause of the row that night, when the lousy bastard Ferriter came spying on us. Ye see, she wrote to me when she came back with this fellah Boulter.'

He got to his feet, stood for a few moments with downcast head and opened mouth and then began to walk aimlessly around the room, his arms hanging loose by his sides.

'This is a nice kettle of fish,' he muttered, 'and a bloke can do nothing about it. I'm caught in a trap.'

Suddenly he looked at Lavan, who had been watching him closely.

'You think I did it, Jack,' he cried. 'But I'm innocent. How in the name o' God am I going to prove it, though?'

'Sit down and tell your story quietly,' said Lavan.

'I prefer to stand,' said O'Leary, continuing to walk about. 'I hardly knew her when I met her again. She had become a regular whore, a proper tough nut, drinking all the time and still she was the same as ever. Aye, it was only the outside of her that had gone wrong, turned hard like a stone, and no wonder after the way she had been used. You know what I mean. There are worse whores living respectable in Merrion Square than in the kips. It's all wrong, the way things are run. This fellah Boulter was some English pimp she had picked up and brought over here to get my goat, a racecourse tout that had done time. He was mixed up in some crooked stunt with Sweep tickets. Then he buzzed off and left her. I believe he's locked up now in Liverpool. When she wrote to me I came to see her. It got my dander up when I saw what she had turned into. I refused to have anything to do with her. She started on the game here in Dublin, and I thought that was a bit too much, coming back here under my very nose and shouting my name to the very dogs in the gutter. She threatened to go before the old man and lay the whole case before him. The kid had been put away in some family of Quakers.'

'Then there was a child?' said Lavan.

'Still is,' said O'Leary. 'Raised as a bloody Protestant. She threw that in my face, too. Then I tried to get the letters off her. She refused. We had an argument and I hit her in the face with the flat of my hand. Honest to God, that was the only time I raised my hand to her. I got sorry afterwards and rang her up. Then we got friendly again. Since that night there was no more hard words between us. May I be struck dead if I'm telling a lie.'

He leaned over the desk, struck it a violent blow with his fist and said in a loud voice:

'God! D'ye think I'm an Italian, to stab a woman in the back? Eh?'

'Certainly not,' said Lavan. 'But tell me, did Mrs. Boulter. . . .'

'That's not her name. Teresa Burke is her name.'

'Well! Did she say anything to you about Ferriter?'

'Ferriter!' cried O'Leary in a furious tone. 'I'll murder that rat.'

Then he struck his palms together with great force and cried aloud:

'That's the fellah that did it. I declare to God it is. He did it on purpose to get me blamed. Why in the name of . . .'

He stared at Lavan with open mouth for a moment or two. Then he swore, grabbed his hat from the chair and jumped to his feet. He shook his clenched fist and cried in a murderous voice:

'I'll get him.'

He ran towards the door. Lavan jumped to his feet and cried:

'Halt that man. Don't let him out.'

O'Leary opened the door and then drew back, finding himself confronted by an armed detective in the corridor outside. He returned to the desk, looking in wonder at Lavan, who had now become a very fierce little man, very stiff and erect, with flashing eyes.

'Sit down,' said Lavan. 'You think because you know me that you can do what you like. That's not correct. I'll lock you up if you carry on like this. You have uttered a threat to murder Ferriter. That's so. And you're quite capable of doing so in your present mood. That's correct. Now pull yourself together and sit down.'

O'Leary jammed his hat viciously on his head

99

and slouched back into his chair, where he sat in a heap, breathing heavily.

'Now do what you please,' he said in a surly voice.

'Tell me whether Teresa Burke ever mentioned anything to you about Ferriter,' said Lavan.

'Go and find out,' said O'Leary. 'I can be just as snotty as you are. Lock me up if you like. But I tell you I'll crack that fellah's skull if I get a chance.'

'Very well, then,' said Lavan sharply. 'I'll lock you up. That'll cool your temper.'

'Hold on, Jack,' cried O'Leary in a different tone. 'Give us a chance. I didn't mean what I said. You don't think I'd dirty my hands with that rat, do you?'

'Very well, then,' said Lavan. 'Be quick about it. Was there something she said about him?'

'There was a whole mouthful,' said O'Leary. 'The night I hit her, she was a bit tight, and he had to help her to her room from the bathroom. It appears she made up to him. Tess was that sort when she got tight, she'd make up to a tom-cat, if there was nothing better handy. But he put the fear of God crosswise in her. So she told me. He started to preach her a sermon. That got her goat, and she fairly got to hate him.

She didn't trust holy fellahs like him since she was at a convent and got into trouble over a priest. She was sacked from the convent. The priest tried to get around her, or so she told me.'

'You can leave that out,' said Lavan angrily. 'I don't want to know what she told you about priests and convents.'

'Listen,' said O'Leary in an appealing tone, 'I didn't mean anything nasty. God forgive me, I thought it would be a good joke to seduce the little devil, so I set her after him.'

'I'm afraid your idea of a joke is very extraordinary,' said Lavan. 'Very queer indeed. You're a fine ornament to your profession in a Catholic country, Dr. O'Leary.'

'Aw! For God's sake, Jack, don't start preaching a sermon. Why don't you have a look at yourself in a mirror some time and laugh? You asked me to tell you what there was between them and I'm telling you.'

'You've told me enough to get yourself in pretty hot water in any case,' said Lavan. 'For your amusement you tried to ruin this young man's immortal soul. Now describe your movements last night and be quick about it.'

'Oh! Well!' said O'Leary with a sigh of despair. 'I knew it was all up with me. The very minute Callahan opened his mouth I knew I was a goner. But I didn't do it. I left the house at two o'clock this morning. She saw me out by the back door and that was the last I saw of her.'

'You left there at two o'clock.'

'I heard it strike two in O'Connell Street a few minutes later.'

'And she saw you out by the back door.'

'That's right.'

'That'll do for the present. Wait outside. Sergeant, tell Guard Stanley to take Dr. O'Leary to the waiting room and send in Mrs. Kelly.'

O'Leary opened his mouth to speak, but instead of doing so, he shrugged his shoulders, got to his feet and waddled out of the room like a sailor. Lavan called Assistant-Commissioner Vesey over the telephone.

'I'd like to see you at once, sir, about this murder,' he said. 'I'm thinking of making an arrest, and I want your advice. What's that? I see. I see. There's sure to be trouble. I see. Ferriter must have told Corish. Could you possibly come down here? Yes. O'Leary is here with me now. All right. I'll keep him here.'

As he hung up the receiver, he heard voices raised in argument outside. A woman's voice was saying:

'Don't you dare lay a hand on me, Sergeant. I won't budge another yard, unless ye let him come in along with me. No. I won't budge. Hang on to me, Jerry. Face them like a man. Not another inch, Sergeant.'

The sergeant came to the door and said:

'She refuses to come in without her husband, sir.'

'Very well. Bring them both in here.'

'Very good, sir. Come on, you two. Look sharp.'

CHAPTER VII

HOLDING one another by the waist, Mrs. Kelly and her husband entered the room. In the struggle with the police, Mrs. Kelly's hat had been knocked to one side. Her hair streamed down over her face and her black eyes shone ferociously. Mr. Kelly, obviously ashamed of his position, rolled his eyes like a negro. His jacket was about his neck and his shirt had been pulled up in front. They separated a little when they arrived before the desk and looked about them sheepishly.

'What's all the row about, Mrs. Kelly?' said Lavan.

'Beg your pardon, sir,' said Mrs. Kelly. 'It's this way. Speak up, Jerry.'

Jerry started, coughed, and took a pace forward. He was a cocky little man, erect and stiff as a poker, obviously an old soldier. About fifty years of age, his chest and stomach had reversed the order of their importance, for although he held himself puffed, with his chin so taut against his throat that little waves of flesh ran slanting on either side of his neck, he seemed to be doing the military gymnastic exercise called 'backwards bend,' from the way his round belly bulged against his belt. He stood to attention, his hands against the seams of his trousers, the toes of his polished shoes pointing outwards at the correct angle. A heavy, grey moustache, carefully clipped and stained brown with beer and tobacco adorned his mottled face. His faded blue eyes bulged as a result of heavy drinking. A grey tweed cap, the crown made stiff by wire, lay far back on his grey head, the peak pointing upwards over a thick bunch of curls that crowded above his forehead. He wore grey flannel trousers, new, clean, well creased, and a blue coat that was shiny at the elbows.

'It's like this, sir,' he began.

'Arrange your dress,' said Lavan.

'Lord save us, look at the cut of ye,' cried Mrs. Kelly.

She laid violent hands on the protruding corner of the shirt and pushed it rudely into its proper position, while Jerry made helpless gestures of protest. Then again he returned to an attitude of military dignity.

'Now speak to the superintendent,' said Mrs. Kelly.

'You start off, Lil,' said Jerry.

'Ye coward, ye promised me to speak,' said Mrs. Kelly.

'What's all this about?' said Lavan.

'It's about us two, sir,' said Mrs. Kelly.

'Wait a minute,' said Jerry. 'I'll tell him.'

He took a tiny pace forward, clicked his heels and began:

'My name is Jeremiah Kelly, late Munster Fusiliers, discharged with the rank of corporal after twenty-one years' service, not a mark of any kind against me. I have a special letter of recommendation for civilian employment from Colonel Sir Maurice. . . .'

'You're Mrs. Kelly's husband, are you?'

'Not according to law, sir.'

'That's right, Jerry. Put it the best way ye can. We meant no harm, sir. It's how we were drove to it.'

'How do you mean?' said Lavan.

'I was married before, sir,' said she.

'Hold on,' said Jerry, nudging her.

'He deserted me, sir,' said Mrs. Kelly excitedly. 'Don't nudge me, Jerry. He ran away from his ship in America, Johnny Corcorcan did, and he was never heard of again.'

'No tale or tidings of him, sir,' said Jerry, 'this twelve years.'

'So?' said Lavan. 'Then you two are living together. That's what you mean.'

'That's right, sir,' said Jerry. 'It's irregular.'

'Oh! Ye won't get us into any harm, sir,' cried Mrs. Kelly. 'I told Jerry we had better come forward, so he says to me. . . .'

'I decided to come forward, sir,' said Jerry in a sing-song voice, 'and make a statement to the effect that this woman, lawfully Mrs. John Corcoran, and me are living in a state of co-habitation.'

'Can we be had up for it, sir?' said Mrs. Kelly.

'Did you go through a form of marriage?' said Lavan.

'No, sir,' said Jerry.

Then the two of them began to speak simultaneously, until finally Lavan ordered them to keep quiet and answer his questions.

'You are the caretaker at . . .' he began.

'Only me, sir,' said Mrs. Kelly.

'I'm employed by a firm of turf accountants on the quays,' said Jerry.

'You mean you tout for a bookmaker.'

'No, sir.'

'I know him,' said the sergeant. 'He works in Jack Riley's S.P. office. He puts up the lists of starters.'

'Now, Mrs. Kelly, tell me all you know about Teresa Burke,' said Lavan.

'Teresa Burke, sir?' said Mrs. Kelly, opening her mouth very wide.

'Look sharp,' said Lavan.

'Beg you pardon, sir,' said Jerry. 'She had no intention to evade the law. But there were others in it. No names no pack drills.'

'There were others in what?'

'Yes, sir,' said Mrs. Kelly. 'I didn't want to speak when you asked me who came to see her, because they were all gentlemen, and I didn't want them to get into any trouble.'

'Who were all gentlemen?'

She mentioned a number of people, including Dr. O'Leary, a District Justice of note, a well-known racehorse owner and a literary personage.

'Were you aware that these men visited her secretly for immoral purposes?'

The couple held council with one another for a few moments, as to which was to answer this question. Finally Jerry decided to speak.

'There was no evidence of immorality, sir,' said Jerry. 'We had no cog . . . cogis . . . cognition of any immoral connivance.'

'What the devil are you talking about?'

'He means to say, sir. . . .'

'Shut your mouth, Lil. Among the gentlemen who called on her was Mr. Rogers and he's Miss Bohan's nephew, he's heir to the property. I mean to say that she owns the house among others.'

'Who owns the house?'

'Miss Bohan. He is her nephew, young Mr. Rogers. He used to come there, so that relieved us of all responsibility, as we are his servants in a way, seeing he sometimes collects the rent and gives us orders. He more or less manages the property. We were placed in a difficult position in the matter. If we complained, we might get the sack, on account of young Mr. Rogers. If we didn't complain, and as we didn't complain, here we are, sir, on the carpet.'

'They were all respectably married men, sir,' said Mrs. Kelly, 'except Dr. O'Leary, so we thought there was no harm done, as they were gentlemen. It's not for a poor person to pass remarks on the goings on of the gentry. If it was poor people, or rowdies that came, I'd have known at once the goings on were immoral.'

'Well! Well!' said Lavan. 'This is a nice state of affairs.'

'Nobody made any complaint about it except

Mr. Ferriter and he was complaining about everything.'

'What did he say?'

'He said no end o' things, sir,' she said, 'the ungrateful ruffian, and me that was like a mother to him. But I think he's out of his mind, the way I often found him sitting there in his room, gaping like a fool. He often terrified the life out of me. Indeed I wouldn't put it past him to murder her himself.'

'None o' that, Lil,' said Jerry. 'No allegations.'

'An' didn't he make allegations against me,' cried Mrs. Kelly furiously, 'saying I was running a brothel, saving your presence, sir? The wicked way he talked about that poor creature, that had no harm to her, only being foolish and led astray. God have mercy on her, she was that pretty, it would bring a tear to yer eye to see her going on the way she was, drinking an' taking no care of herself.'

'You were friendly with her. Did she ever speak to you about Dr. O'Leary or about any quarrel she had with him?'

'She didn't say much to me about Dr. O'Leary, but I know they were fond of one another, from the olden times. It was about the other lad she talked to me.'

'About Ferriter?'

'Yes. She was afraid of him. He threatened her one night, saying he'd expose her, that's what she said and get her run out of the country and then, God forgive her, she used to make fun of him and that made him wild. Only a week ago she said to me: "Mrs. Kelly," says she, "I'm getting afraid of that man, the awful looks he gives me whenever I meet him." He belongs to a society, sir, that watches people and reports goings on. She said to me he was one of those people that want something for nothing and when they can't get it, don't want anybody else to have it.'

'What did she mean by that?'

'I don't know, sir.'

'We wish to make no allegations against him,' said Jerry. 'He's a clean living man and he belongs to a confraternity and a sodality as well as this other society that watches people.'

In answer to Lavan's questions they both made rambling statements about their movements on the previous night. Mrs. Kelly said that she vaguely heard the back door being closed at some early hour of the morning, but she could not say whether one person or two persons went to the back door. She just heard the door close and fell asleep again. The noise did not disturb her, as it often happened that Teresa Burke let people out that way during the night.'

'Well! Now,' said Lavan, 'which of you opened the door this morning? I mean the back door.'

'I did, sir,' said Jerry. 'I was awakened by the screaming of Miss Beamish and I ran out into the area to see what was the matter.'

'How did you find the door? Bolted or not?'

Jerry Kelly thought for a moment and said he found it bolted.

'Now think carefully.'

'It was bolted, sir.'

'Are you prepared to swear it was bolted?'

'Yes, sir,' he said. 'I'm prepared to swear it was bolted.'

At that moment the examination was cut short by sounds of a violent commotion taking place outside.

CHAPTER VIII

FERRITER had rushed from the office of the *Morning Star* to police headquarters in a state of great excitement, muttering to himself that he was going to put an end to all doubt as to the identity of the culprit. The wretched man was now convinced that O'Leary had killed the woman and that there was a conspiracy to saddle himself with the murder. He entered the building and was walking up to the desk, when he heard a shout. Turning his head, he saw O'Leary coming towards him.

Staggered by the apparition of this man, whom he was certain could not be anywhere near, he opened his mouth and held up his hands like a prisoner surrendering in battle.

'Help,' he cried. 'He's going to kill me.'

At the next moment, O'Leary closed with him, gripping him fiercely by the throat with both hands, yelling as he did so:

'It's your turn now, you dirty rat.'

Ferriter closed his eyes, afraid to look on the terrible face of his enemy. Then he lost consciousness. When he came to his senses a few minutes later, he found himself in a chair, a detective holding him by the shoulders, while a uniformed sergeant held a glass of water to his lips. Across the room he saw O'Leary, still struggling and shouting, manacled and pinioned by two detectives. Lavan was standing in front of O'Leary, saying something and pointing his finger.

'I'll get him yet,' screamed O'Leary, trying to escape from the detectives.

As he sipped the water, Ferriter felt very pleased, and for the first time since he had plunged the knife he was able to pray to God with success. He gave thanks that his enemy was in custody. There were manacles on his hands and he was a prisoner.

'Put this man in a cell,' said Lavan sharply.

'Ha!' thought Ferriter. 'Then all is well with me. I can now begin my attack. On Corish, too. I'll expose that vulgar ruffian. I'll expose them all. I'll spare nobody.'

He was trembling like a leaf and it seemed that his throat was too swollen for him to breathe, but he felt full of enthusiasm and courage. As O'Leary was being led away, the uniformed sergeant said to Lavan:

'He'd have strangled him in another second. Before we knew what had happened he jumped up and made a dive at him, like a tiger. He has powerful strength in his arms.'

'He can amuse himself with the door of his cell,' said Lavan. 'Are you badly hurt, Mr. Ferriter?'

'I wanted to speak to you,' said Ferriter, struggling to his feet and smiling faintly, 'but I see that the man is already in custody.'

Lavan looked at him sharply and said:

'Come this way.'

He took Ferriter by the arm and led him along the passage. On the way they passed Mrs. Kelly and her husband. Feriter looked at them vaguely and then felt a thrill of pleasure, as he remembered that they were also going to pay the penalty for their misdeeds, as being morally responsible for the crime.

'Well!' said Lavan, when he had placed Ferriter in a chair before his desk. 'Was it something you forgot to tell me this morning?'

Ferriter looked up at the superintendent, smiling with pleasure. He felt grateful towards Lavan as towards a protector.

'Something happened since I saw you last.' he said, 'that convinced me I must rely entirely on you to see that justice is done. I have been sacked from my job.'

He expected this pronouncement to have a strong effect on Lavan, and he was considerably surprised to see that Lavan's expression did not change in the least. He merely nodded his head slightly, pursed up his lips and said in his shrewd, cold voice:

'So? You have lost your job. That's so. Why did you lose it?'

Ferriter was a trifle awed by this tone and by the way Lavan was looking at him. Lavan's bright blue eyes were now very fierce and hostile. His lips curled slightly and his nose kept twitching. His forehead was lined. He was leaning against the side of the desk, tapping the edges with his fingers and staring intently into Ferriter's face. His eyes darted hither and thither over Ferriter's face, now resting on the mouth, now on the chin, now on the forehead, now on the cheeks, as if they were taking measurements. Under this inspection, which was strange and unexpected, Ferriter did not lose his confidence, but he lost the feeling of being under Lavan's protection. So his insolence returned.

'I must remind him . . .' he said to himself.

But of what should he remind him? Even at

116

that moment of supreme confidence, generated by the sight of O'Leary's manacled hands, a little serpent, red and twisted like a germ of disease, appeared in his mind. And he remembered how uncouth the plunged dagger looked and how he had struggled to drag it forth, all covered with frothing blood. Thrust rudely forward in escape from this serpent, he cried out insolently:

'Mr. Corish, the editor of the *Morning Star*, sacked me because I told him what O'Leary had to do with this murder. And I now want to tell you that I am convinced that O'Leary murdered her. I am prepared to swear it in court. He was responsible for the murder, not only last night, but for the past eight years he has been responsible. She told me with her own lips, that night I found her in the bathroom, that he ruined her, crushed her and threw her away and then returned like a dog on his vomit to devour what was left.'

He had spoken very rapidly, and his words were barely understandable, owing to the way his shark-like jaws protruded in excitement.

'Yes, yes,' Lavan said hurriedly, eager for him to continue in this state.

Ferriter got to his feet and cried out:

'I also denounce as responsible for this murder, Mr. Corish, editor of the *Morning Star*, for refusing to expose in his newspaper the immorality that is going on here. I denounce the Government and the whole community for the gross materialism and the base pursuit of wealth and pleasure, which pollutes our streets and our houses with the foulness of sin. I call on you as a just man, if you value your immortal soul and your responsibility to God for the trust that has been placed in you, to drag these criminals forth into the light and expose them. Let this murder be a sign, like the destruction of Sodom and Gomorrah. How many just men shall we find here? One or two are sufficient. The rest shall shrink from them in terror and then . . .'

'One moment,' said Lavan sharply. 'Do you want to prefer a charge against Dr. O'Leary?'

'I prefer a charge of murder against him,' said Ferriter.

'You can't do that,' said Lavan. 'You are still alive. He certainly threatened to murder you. You can charge him with assault and with uttering threats but . . .'

'I'm not talking about myself,' cried Ferriter, almost in a shout. 'Have you not arrested him for the murder?'

'Do you or do you not want to bring a charge against him for the assault he made on you just now? Leave the murder out of it for the moment.'

Suddenly, Ferriter sat down and went limp. He licked his dry lips and his head swam. He began to mutter vaguely. Lavan came forward, held out his hand and said:

'Did you make a statement to Mr. Corish somewhat similar to what you made to me just now?'

Ferriter looked up, scared like a cur over which a whip is held.

'What statement,' he muttered.

'Did you ask him to denounce certain people and conditions? Speak up. You have no reason to look afraid. Why should you be afraid? You have committed no crime, have you? Why should you be afraid when I ask you what you said to Mr. Corish?'

'Yes,' whispered Ferriter, 'I asked Mr. Corish to do more or less what I ask you now. But he is sold to the enemy.'

'What enemy?'

Ferriter looked around the room in pain and shrugged his shoulders.

'I have nobody with me,' he said pathetically. 'Nobody believes.'

'What enemy?' repeated Lavan sharply.

'Mammon,' said Ferriter in a low whisper.

'Then you went at once to Mr. Corish,' said Lavan, 'with a fixed plan.'

Ferriter started and became rigid.

'Who said anything about a plan?' he cried angrily.

'You must have had a scheme,' said Lavan. 'It won't do you any good to get excited. Otherwise I'll begin to suspect that you are concealing something. You have told me already that you knew this murder was going to happen.'

'What if I did?'

'Instead of going to the police or doing something to prevent it. . . .'

Again Ferriter jumped to his feet and cried out fiercely:

'What good would that be? Who pays any attention to me? Has anybody ever paid any attention to me? Haven't I been ridiculed and offended all my life? Is it my fault that God didn't make me strong in body? Is there no respect for the intelligence? If I am sensitive and if I believe in something higher, must I be despised and made a laughing stock? What happened when I went to the committee? He is a rich man's son, so they protect him. The others are prosperous libertines and they go free. She is a damned soul and even her spilt blood does not redeem her.'

'Sit down,' cried Lavan. His eyes were now dancing. 'You expected this murder and for some reason — I must say it's a queer one — you had a plan ready, to expose people. That's so. You went to Mr. Corish with it. That's correct. He sacked you. Then you came to me. I turn it down too. That's correct. Do you understand?'

Ferriter and Lavan were now standing face to face, their breasts almost touching. It seemed to Ferriter that Lavan was trying to force him back with his eyes, to throw him down on his back and then grope in through his eyes into his mind in order to discover what was there. It seemed there was a weight pushing him and trying to force him down, and although the effort was great he resisted this weight. He met Lavan's eyes with a desperate courage.

'I understand you,' he whispered. 'You are with the rest. They pay you. You are their servant. I see I can expect nothing from you.'

'You might get what you don't expect,' said Lavan. 'I'm getting suspicious of your plans and of your habits. You are mighty cute. That's so,

But you're not the only one that's cute. If you're going to be smart with me, you may be sorry for it.'

'I don't fear you,' said Ferriter softly. 'I'm not afraid. You can't make me afraid.'

'Do you know that the back door was locked on the inside this morning?' said Lavan, also softly. 'Did you know that? Eh?'

Ferriter's eyes opened very wide and then they almost closed. That monstrous desire to strike down and kill came upon him and his head immediately became clouded, as if it were surrounded with a thick fog. He could barely see Lavan's eyes through this fog. Then he heard the man say in the same low voice:

'And you hardly ever smoke? Do you? Hardly ever?'

The cloud vanished. Lavan had taken a pace to the rear and folded his arms.

'Jesus, Mary and Joseph,' said Ferriter to himself, 'I offer you up my heart and soul. Holy Saint Francis, protect me.'

He put his hand to his forehead and then sat down. Lavan lit a cigarette and said in a different voice:

'That's why I don't think I'll help you to carry out your scheme. Not that I think much of it in any case. I respect my religion, but I'm not that sort of a man. Judge not and you shall not be judged. How would you like to be judged yourself, Mr. Ferriter? I'm not talking of the sentence and the black cap — extremely horrible ceremony it must be, I've seen a few — but of something different. You hear people talking of the advantage of a sudden death, drowning and so on, head carried away by a shell; but I am of the opinion that even instant death is a terrible wrench and that a person suffers the same agony as a long-drawn-out death.'

Ferriter looked slowly around the room and noticed for the first time that there were several people there besides Lavan. They were all watching him strangely. He grew cunning. Putting his hand to his throat, he began to groan, muttering that O'Leary had hurt him. While he was doing so, he thought very rapidly, planning how he was going to make his escape from the police house. He was now aware that Lavan definitely suspected him and was trying to force him to incriminate himself by mental torture. He must outwit that contemptible policeman by superior cunning. In a flash the idea came to him. Pretending to be in hysteria, he put his head in his hands and cried:

'God forgive me! I see I was wrong to judge anybody. Why should I get mixed up with them in any case? My mother told me I should have left that place, when I told her what was going on there. Now I have ruined myself, lost my job and made enemies of all these people. O my God! I feel so ill. What am I to do now? I don't want to make anybody unhappy, but it seems that everything I do must be wrong. I only wanted to do what I thought was my duty, superintendent. I take it all back. I don't want to accuse anybody.'

He went on talking in this rambling fashion for some time before he realized that something had happened in the room. Looking up, he saw that Lavan had gone. The others were still watching him. He got to his feet, intending to leave the room, when one of the detectives motioned him to sit down.

'What's that?' said Ferriter vaguely, still pretending to be hysterical.

'Sit down, please,' said the detective.

Ferriter sat down and put his head in his hands. Now he felt very tired. He did not want to struggle any further. The idea came to him that it would be more noble to confess and read his manuscript from the dock. In his exhaustion, this idea made him morbidly happy. He began to picture the consternation of the judge, the jury and the audience. He saw the newsboys rushing through the streets with the newspapers telling of the extraordinary statement made by the accused man. But when it came to the black cap, he shuddered and put away the idea. Then he began again to rehearse the scheme. He was disturbed in his second rehearsal by the entrance of Lavan, who was followed by Assistant-Commissioner Vesey.

Mr. Vesey rather resembled Lavan in body, but his face was quite different, being much more intellectual and refined. His face looked very gentle and kind. His eyes were particularly fine, being of a grey colour and very luminous. His hair was going grey at the temples and he wore a little moustache. He saluted Ferriter, whom he knew fairly well. Ferriter got to his feet and came forward to shake hands with him; but being amazed that Mr. Vesey did not take his hands from the pockets of his jacket, although he kept smiling, Ferriter halted at a distance of a few feet and dropped his outstretched hand. He found it very disturbing that Mr. Vesey kept his hands in the pockets of his jacket.

'I believe you are in some sort of trouble here,

Mr. Ferriter,' said the commissioner. 'Mr. Lavan was telling me something. . . .'

His voice drifted away and he looked aside, as if he were shy of being in the room, in the presence of all these people, with whom he had no real connection. This was partly the case. A man of the highest integrity and gifted with great talents, he had served with distinction in the Imperial army during the Great War, attaining the rank of general. He had also served with distinction in the Free State army during the Civil War and then entered the police, where he was exceedingly popular among all classes, in spite of the heightened feelings that are only natural in a generation like ours, when brother has fought brother. Yet he was essentially not a policeman, in spite of his capacity for organization and his love of order. Ruthless when absolutely necessary, his mild nature was revolted by force or cruelty of any kind. He was equally repelled by the religious fanaticism which is part of our unfortunate legacy from civil strife and the frustration of our political ambitions. Indeed, he was prominent in every attempt to encourage painting and the drama. For that reason he disliked people of Ferriter's type.

'I've got myself into a whole lot of trouble,' cried Ferriter, 'through my own foolishness. I wanted to oblige the superintendent there and told him all I knew about this murder, and then I've been sacked from my job as a result. Now I'm being . . .'

'So?' said Lavan. 'That's something new.'

'Just a moment,' said Mr. Vesey. 'You were going to say . . .'

'I'm being bullied here,' said Ferriter. 'I was attacked by Dr. O'Leary, and now I'm being tormented. I ask you to protect me.'

'Of course,' said Mr. Vesey. 'What are you being bullied about?'

'The superintendent has been making certain insinuations.'

'I see. What were they?'

Then Ferriter blurted out:

'I don't care what happens. I'm going to see that everybody responsible is exposed. I refuse to be silenced. Not even you, Mr. Vesey, if you adopt that attitude. I'm not afraid. You can't hold me here.'

'Who is holding you here?'

'Nobody is holding him here,' said Lavan. 'He came of his own accord. We didn't bring him here.'

'Then why have you set a man following me?' cried Ferriter.

'Who said there was a man following you?' cried Lavan.

'You can't deny it,' said Ferriter. 'That little fellow. I'm sure he's following me. It's persecution. I'm not going to stand for it. And you can't hold me here either.'

'You may go at any moment you please,' said the commissioner calmly. 'There's the door. Nobody'll stop you. Well?'

Ferriter stood undecided, terrified as much by their willingness to let him go, as he had been by the fear that they would hold him. Then he suddenly rushed forward. His legs swayed under him and his feet itched, until he got outside the door. Then he felt relieved.

The commissioner and Lavan looked at one another.

'Don't touch him yet,' said Mr. Vesey. 'He'll hang himself if he's guilty. The more you leave him alone the better. Just keep a good eye on him. There's plenty of time before this evening. Have his room well searched and find out everything you can about him. But don't pull him until you have something definite to go on. You never know with a bird like that. He might get as obstinate as a mule if you try to rush him. They can be courageous enough when they're desperate and as cunning as foxes. It's uncertainty he fears. Carry on.'

CHAPTER IX

On leaving the police headquarters, Ferriter
went to see his mother, who was staying at his
sister's house in Rathmines. Lately he had not
seen very much of his mother. She disapproved
of his life and they had become a trifle estranged;
failing to understand one another. Yet, at this
moment, such trifles seemed to him of no account.
He wanted someone to sympathize with him and
protect him. Naturally nobody could do that
as well as his mother. So it seemed to him. He
got on a Rathmines tram, after looking carefully
in all directions to see whether he was being
followed.

He was now fully conscious of being a hunted
man, conscious of being a murderer, conscious
that the whole of society was waiting to pounce
on him for the crime he had committed. It was
an astounding feeling. Often, while he was
planning the murder, he had imagined what
this would be like, but had never imagined anything like the reality. It had always appeared
in some manner majestic and awe-inspiring, like

thunder or the roar of battle; but now the only thunder was the threat in the dark sky, where clouds were massing, lying heavy over the earth, sagging bellies swaying in the firmament. Within himself there was no thunder, just a queer terror that kept his nerves on edge and made him envy greedily the man who handed him his tram-ticket. Oh! How wonderful it would be to change places with that man and to be free from terror! When the tram jolted he shuddered. The bursting of a motor tyre in the distance made him leap from his seat. He felt sure that an old gentleman opposite was a detective, simply because the man glanced sharply over his newspaper. What was he reading? An account of the murder? All had vanished now from his mind except the fear of pursuit. Mr. Vesey had kept his hands in his pockets and Lavan had said the back door was locked on the inside. Then they knew already. Perspiration began to ooze from his forehead. He tore his ticket into fragments, and as the car was rounding the Green at the top of Grafton Street he jumped down and changed into a bus. There he grew calm, feeling that he had evaded his pursuers. He bent down, pretending to tie his shoe-lace and felt his shins, where the manuscript and the photograph were hidden within his socks. If he had only got rid of them! Now there was such a multitude of things to be constantly remembered; so many trivial things that it was impossible to concentrate his mind on the things that were important, the majesty of God shining forth upon a regenerated world. He was in a state of panic when he reached his sister's house.

Six years previously his sister Agnes, who was four years his senior, had married Professor Anthony Mellett, a man of considerable reputation in Dublin as an authority on the liver. Agnes had met him at the university, where she had a successful career and was looked upon as a woman of talent, with rather advanced views. She really had not much talent and her views, if she had any at all, were merely a pose to attract the professor. She possessed to a very high degree that feminine quality of imitation and repetition, which so often gives a false value to a woman's intellect. In any case, she managed to impose on Mr. Mellett by affecting to share his views, and he was so pleased that he married her. He regarded himself as a man of extreme views. Indeed there had been some talk at one time of his having to resign his seat owing to his views, as it was considered dangerous that a man who was suspected of not believing in the Immaculate Conception should hold a position of responsibility in a Catholic university. The professor's opinions were undoubtedly sincere. Agnes, in holding the same opinions and in desiring to marry him, was merely inspired by vanity and an ambition to improve her social position. The professor was accepted among the Protestant intelligentsia as a man of consequence, and she thought also to curry favour with them on her own account by sneering at the modes of thought of her own people, the Catholic middle class, which has assumed political power without having as yet attained a corresponding degree of social importance.

This characteristic, a sort of inferiority complex, was present also in Ferriter, although in a different form. Whereas his sister toadied to the class which they both instinctively felt to be superior, Ferriter was driven by a feeling of shame for his antecedents into a violent hatred of that class, so that he became a social failure and a religious fanatic. Although in his own upbringing he had never suffered the sting of poverty, he never got over the consciousness that his paternal grandfather had been a farm labourer, who set up as a huckster, collected a little money, married a humble woman who had a little more money and so was able to buy a public house and send his son to college. And this son married the daughter of a country shop-keeper, whose people were also of the soil, serfs of the old order. For two generations they had been crawling up to affluence, escaping from the soil and from serfdom; but somehow the soil had clung to them in the shape of the growling, envious mass that had been left behind, or exploited to permit the rise of a few individuals from the herd. On the other hand, the ranks of the old bourgeoisie were closed in a menacing and insulting fashion against the newcomers. Ferriter turned back in disgust from this latter group and yet could not return to his roots, which he found crude and repulsive. His family, regarding this attitude as treasonable to their am-bition, had recently become antagonistic to him.

This was especially the case with his mother. Her husband's bankruptcy and death had been a great blow to her. Since that time she had wandered about, staying with her married children, complaining about her bad health and the injustice of the world. She always referred to her late husband as 'poor Peter, God forgive him.' He had committed an unpardonable offence in the eyes of such upstart people by dying without leaving any property. One of her sons was a doctor in London. Another was a district justice in a southern county. A daughter had become a nun. Agnes had married an eminent professor. Together with Aunt Mary, her husband's sister and the wife of a Cabinet Minister — all these children settled respectably in life would have made void the scandal of 'poor Peter's' death were it not for the failure and folly of Francis.

Therefore, when Francis rang the bell at the professor's door, he was anxious about his reception. He found the family at lunch. The servant was just clearing away the soup, and the professor, with a large nakpin hanging from his neck, was standing up, about to carve a leg of mutton. The two eldest of the professor's four children, a pair of twin boys aged five, sat at the bottom of the table, one on either side of Mrs. Ferriter. One of them was crying at that moment, having slobbered something over his napkin. He was being cleaned by Agnes. Nobody took any serious notice of Ferriter's arrival, except the twin who was not crying.

'You sent me nothing for my birthday, Uncle Frank,' said this twin.

'Hello, Frank!' said Agnes. 'You musn't say things like that, Sean. Uncle Frank has no money to buy toys.'

'Bring another plate, Jenny,' said the professor. 'Have some lunch, Frank. Glad you came.'

Mrs. Ferriter wiped her mouth with a napkin and then held up her mouth to be kissed.

'You came out without your coat,' she said, 'and I'm sure it's going to rain. You should take more care of yourself or you'll be down again with sickness. It's not when you're sick you want to take care but before it. But it's a waste of breath giving you advice.'

She was a plump woman of fifty, with a ruddy face, very fond of food.

'I've something much more serious to think about at this moment.' said Ferriter, going to his chair.

Agnes looked at him closely and said:

'You don't look well. Are you working too hard? How are you getting on with your writing?'

Agnes resembled her mother in appearance and character. She had furthermore the aggressiveness that is typical of our generation, no doubt a product of the violent upheaval caused by the revolution, the anger of a class that has been enslaved for centuries and is eager to parade its freedom in a harsh manner. She was a full-busted woman, with strong hips and very straight, fair hair, which she insisted on trying to curl. Her teeth were slightly stained with nicotine.

'If you don't behave yourself, Brian,' said the professor, 'you'll leave the table.'

The twin who had just stopped crying began again to cry at this remark, but the professor brandished his napkin and the twin became silent. The professor put his napkin again to his neck and sharpened his knife with a great flourish. He was a man of forty-five, tall and uncouth, spare of frame, with large awkward limbs and a pronounced stoop, as is common with very tall men, unless they are soldiers or such-like professionals. He had high cheekbones and hollow cheeks. He was so dark in complexion that he looked unshaven, even though his chin shone from the razor. His hair was black, but it had gone grey at the temples. His eyebrows were also black and very thick. A black mous-tache, which drooped over the sides of his lips in walrus fashion, especially gave his face a for-bidding look. His clothes were clumsily made and untidy. As he carved the meat, he had repeatedly to pick a pair of pince-nez out of the dish, wherein they had dropped from his nose, but, being attached by a piece of string to the lapel of his coat, were prevented from getting completely lost in the gravy. Every time they fell he mumbled something in an irritated tone, but insisted on putting them again to his nose, although his wife kept on asking him to put them in his pocket.

Although the very thought of food was distasteful to him and he wanted to draw his mother aside into another room and ask her help, Ferriter had sat down and remained silent. Already he felt by the atmosphere that he would receive neither assistance nor sympathy from his mother. Now more than ever, in spite of the terrible position in which he was placed, he felt that she was alien to him. He had drifted away from her beyond the power of returning. He noticed also with humiliation the indifference, almost contempt, with which they all treated his presence. Although it was nearly a month since he had been in the house they made no effort to entertain him. Indeed, except for an occasional word from the twins, silence lasted until Agnes repeated her reference to his writing.

'Have you sold anything since, Frank?' she said.

The family had a vague hope that Ferriter

might become a success as a writer, since he appeared to be good for none of the more profitable professions. He had been offering short stories and articles to various editors for some time, but with no great success, except among the religious publications, which did not pay their contributors.

'I have an article on Round Towers appearing in the *Catholic Vanguard* shortly,' he said without interest.

'Waste of time, Frank,' said the professor, dropping his carving knife and holding out his pince-nez in his right hand, with a little backward shrug of his shoulders, as if he were stressing a point in a lecture. 'They don't pay and they publish drivel. Anything that the *Catholic Vanguard* may publish about Round Towers or about anything else can have no importance whatsoever. If you must write drivel why not get paid for it?'

'I disagree with you,' said Ferriter quietly.

He spoke from habit, although at this moment the professor's taunts did not interest him. Professor Mellett took a perverse delight in giving Ferriter good advice, that perverse pleasure which agnostics get from ragging devout Christians.

'I think you should pay more attention to the advice that is given to you, Frank,' said Mrs. Ferriter, with melancholy unction. 'They pay good money for things that are printed nowadays in novels and magazines. I met a young man in London at George's house and he earns thousands a year writing serials for the newspapers.'

'I'm not a prostitute,' said Ferriter with dignity.

His mother's ignorance always put him to shame.

'Pooh!' said the professor, drawing his hand over his moustache. 'That's a strong word. To make money is not a sign of prostitution.'

'You could hardly call Anatole France a prostitute,' said Agnes. 'He wrote serials for the newspapers.'

'What he wrote does not interest me,' said Ferriter. 'He was an impostor.'

'Pooh!' cried the professor. 'An impostor! One of the great intellects of France an impostor! Ridiculous! It's my personal opinion that more harm is being done to the young intellect of this country by the new gospel of Puritanism, a gospel entirely alien to the genius of our race, than by all the former tyranny of England. Until we eradicate this idea that material prosperity is pernicious we can get nowhere. We'll remain a third class people. The tragedy is that we seek it *sub rosa* and deny it in the high places.'

He fixed his pince-nez savagely to his nose and, having finished carving the mutton, he sat down.

'It's all futile,' cried Ferriter, beginning to get angry, not so much at what the professor was saying, as at the relation this trivial conversation bore to the torture he was suffering inwardly.

'Rot,' said the professor. 'You are going to start the old story of the unhappy millionaire. It's all rot. Have some food. You don't eat enough. As a race we don't eat enough. That's the trouble with us. Too much fasting and tea and bread and butter.'

'It's no harm for anybody to be able to pay his way,' said Mrs. Ferriter. 'I think you shouldn't have given up studying for the bar, Frank. With a little struggle you could have gone on with it and you could work on the *Morning Star* at the same time. I'm sure your brothers George and Michael would have been only too pleased to help you, and you could always get a meal from your sister Agnes.'

Ferriter flushed deeply and then, in an access of mocking despair, he wanted to announce to them that he was a murderer. But the professor continued to speak.

'The bar!' he said, after swallowing a large mouthful of mutton. 'The curse of this country is that the luxury professions are overcrowded. We have too many lawyers and doctors and priests.'

'Quite true,' said Mrs. Mellett.

'We couldn't have too many priests,' said Mrs. Ferriter gently. 'I can't agree with you there, Anthony.'

'Far too many,' said the professor. 'This is becoming a clerical state, I'm afraid. If I might offer you one word of advice, Frank, and it's advice I've offered you once or twice already, you are doing yourself no good by being mixed up with these vigilance societies and busybodies that are turning us into ridicule abroad. It's worse than England after the Cromwellian revolution, when they burned Shakespeare in the public market-place. We are descending to the level of the English, a race notorious for its hypocrisy.'

Recently the professor had become violent against the English, owing to some bad reviews he had received in English scientific papers for a book he had published on the liver.

'Can you deny it?' he cried, amazed that Ferriter made no reply.

'At this moment it does not interest me,' said Ferriter.

'You should listen to his advice, Frank,' said Mrs. Ferriter, chewing greedily. 'You're not eating either. What's the matter with you?'

Ferriter laid down the fork, with which he had been making patterns on the cloth. He flushed deeply. Should he tell them now? No. Not in the presence of the children. They were still pure. Then suddenly he felt malicious.

'The fact is,' he said, 'I'm not at all hungry. I'm much too excited. I came here to ask your advice, but not on the question of my writing.'

'On what question, then, may I ask?' said the professor.

'Shall I tell them right away?' thought Ferriter, looking from his mother to his sister and then to the professor. 'Not yet.'

'It's about a woman that was living in the same house with me,' he said aloud.

'Oh! You're still worried about that woman,' said Agnes with a little laugh. 'Didn't you want to get her a job some time ago? I think you're very silly, Frank.'

'What's all this about a woman?' said Mrs. Ferriter anxiously.

'It's the woman Frank was trying to save,' said Agnes. 'He went around trying to get a job for her and brought her to mass, but she dropped back again. I thought you had lost interest in her, Frank. Are you sure you're not in love with her?'

The two bright red spots appeared on Ferriter's cheeks.

'How can you be so cruel?' he cried, looking at his sister in horror. 'Why must you joke about serious things I tell you? If you only knew how serious these things. . . .'

'There you are again,' said the professor, as he rolled a piece of potato on a fork around his plate to cover it with gravy. 'Eat your mutton. As a race we are much too serious. Jenny, take the children to the kitchen. They are misbehaving themselves. Give them an orange or something. Out you get now. It's quite true. A Swiss gentleman told me he was surprised by the morbid expression of the people he met in the streets of Dublin. It's this new gospel of sackcloth and ashes. I remember this woman you mentioned here one day. She was a . . .'

The professor paused as the servant dragged

the resisting twins out of the door. When the door closed, he continued:

'She was a . . .'

'She was a prostitute,' interrupted Ferriter in a sombre voice, staring fixedly at the table. 'At that time she was a prostitute. She is one no longer.'

This pronouncement was received with amazement. Mrs. Ferriter made the sign of the cross on her forehead and then lowered her eyes, at the mention of something unclean. Agnes looked at her brother, as if she suspected he had gone mad. The professor alone did not seem to be surprised, but he remained argumentative.

'When you say she is a . . .'

'Why don't you say the word?' cried Ferriter angrily.

'I don't belong to the younger generation,' said the professor with dignity. 'There are certain words I refrain from using in the presence of ladies.'

'Oh! Frank,' cried Mrs. Ferriter, almost in tears. 'I told you long ago that was no fit place for you to live, with all the ructions going on there. The last time I went to see you, before you were took ill, I found a heap of dust in a corner of the stairs and that slovenly woman going about. I'm sure she drinks. You must leave it and go to some respectable place.'

'You are trying to tell me that she has reformed,' said the professor. 'I tell you it's impossible. They never reform.'

'Not when they have to deal with a society of people who are without a conception of God,' cried Ferriter.

'What have these wicked women to do with God?' cried Mrs. Ferriter. 'They have no souls.'

'All people made in God's image have souls,' cried Ferriter.

'I detest heat,' cried the professor. 'The whole trouble with us as a race is that we cannot discuss things coldly. That much at least I grant the English.'

Mrs. Ferriter got to her feet and said:

'If you are going to discuss anything of the sort I'm leaving the room.'

Ferriter jumped up and said in a pained tone:

'Don't go, mother. I want to tell you something. It's quite another thing altogether. Please sit down. It concerns everybody.'

'I knew you'd drive me to an early grave with shame and disgrace, Frank,' she said, sitting down again. 'After all the money that was spent on you, sending you to Trinity. It all came from sending you to that Protestant place. Your father, God forgive him, he got wrong ideas into his head when he began to go about with that racing crowd. Now you're taking up with street women. I'll never forgive you. Agnes, you should have told me about it. I'm leaving here in the morning. I'm going to my son George, where I never hear anything about shameful people.'

'I'm terribly sorry,' said Ferriter, 'to bring shame on anybody. It was something else entirely that . . .'

'Pay no attention to mother,' said Agnes. 'She's always like that. If she had some work to do, she wouldn't be so cantankerous.'

'No quarrelling, please,' said the professor.

'I'm not going to quarrel,' said Agnes cheerfully, 'but it's quite true, mother. You're beside yourself because you haven't an opportunity of grumbling about having to work from morning till night looking after a house.'

'I never thought you'd cast it in my face that I'm homeless,' said Mrs. Ferriter tearfully.

'Come, come,' said the professor, 'your mother must be forgiven, Agnes, for taking up an old-fashioned attitude towards the question. Under the matriarchate from which we have suffered in this country — it's quite true Mrs. Ferriter and I mean no offence — we didn't face these questions from a scientific angle. What you must recognize is this, Frank: no matter how you try to hide the fact, prostitution is a necessary evil under our present mode of life. Our institution of marriage — and a very fine institution it is on the whole — is largely for the protection of property, handing down from father to legitimate son, but I have dealt with that in conversation with you already. These wretched women exist as a protection for respectable women, to prevent their being treated with violence, to put it crudely. It's a sad sort of business, but it cannot be helped, and in my opinion their existence should be recognized and regulated by the government. We cannot have sexual violence, which is becoming too frequent since these forcible measures. I think it's very foolish of you to allow yourself to be led astray by sentiment. Let the woman stew in her own juice. You can't save her.'

'Did I say I had saved her?' said Ferriter slowly, looking the professor in the eyes.

'But I thought you said that . . .'

'The woman is dead,' said Ferriter solemnly.

'Indeed!' said the professor a little nervously. 'Upon my soul!'

'Yes,' continued Ferriter still more solemnly. 'She was stabbed to the heart last night in her bedroom and she is dead.'

'Good God!'

The three of them uttered the exclamation simultaneously and Mrs. Ferriter was so astonished that she forgot to make the sign of the cross. Agnes again looked at her brother suspiciously. Ferriter kept his eyes on the table in front of him, and he had begun to tremble at the knees, between which his hands were clasped.

'Oh!' said the professor. 'I heard the newsboys shouting something as I was coming home.'

'My poor boy,' said Mrs. Ferriter, 'have you taken your things away?'

Ferriter looked at his mother, with an appealing look in his eyes. Could she not see? Why could she not see? Why could he not throw himself on his knees before her and bury his head in her lap, howl his sorrow like an infant and get rid of this heavy load that was weighing on him? As he looked at her, he thought he saw understanding in her eyes for a moment; but at the next moment, she dropped her eyes from his, and all contact was lost again. He shuddered.

'How did this happen?' said Agnes.

He looked at his sister's eyes and saw a vague

149

suspicion in them. He remembered that he had never really been intimate with any of his brothers or sisters except with Lily, who was now a nun. All the others were strangers, especially Agnes, She was going to play golf after lunch. How self-possessed and indifferent she looked in her tweed skirt and knitted jumper! An alien! Should he destroy her self-possession by telling her everything right now? Would she care?

Suddenly it occurred to him that none of them would care, not even his mother, except for the disgrace it might bring on them, whether he had murdered the woman through lust, jealousy or the most noble motives. A savage anger mounted to his head.

'How it happened is a long story,' he said fiercely. 'It happened partly the day I came here and asked your help to get this woman a job. But you refused. So did everybody else. You all laughed at me. Now she is dead and you find it interesting. It's news. And they will shield the criminal that is responsible. It's going to be hushed up and the whole affair will just be another brutal murder of a harlot, a few days' horror and nothing more. It's all going to go on as it was before, sin and misery and all of you sneering at everybody that is sane enough to strive for something higher. You mock me because I have no money in the bank. When I went to Aunt Mary and asked her to help this woman she asked me if I had a dinner jacket, so that she could invite me to her dance. I'll go to her now, too, for another reason. I'm going to drag everybody into this. Let the police see that I'm connected with you all. If you are ashamed of me you'll have proper cause for shame. Let me be crucified, but I'll go to the cross as your relative. How do you like that? Are you horrified, mother? You don't understand. It's all Greek to you. Well! I was sacked from my job this morning. You undertsand that.'

He was trembling from head to foot. He had risen to his feet as he spoke, and he now swayed against the table, grasping his fork, point downwards, just as he had grasped the dagger. Then he threw it from him, burst into tears and dropped down into his chair, laying his arms and head on the table.

'Quick, Anthony, do something,' said Agnes. 'He's in a fit.'

Mrs. Ferriter rushed over and threw herself on her son. She began to weep, caressing his head with her hands. He turned around, clutched at her sleeve and pressed his cheek against it. The professor poured out a little brandy into a glass. They made him take a sip. He shook his head and then looked around him in a dazed fashion.

'Oh! What's the matter, Frank?' wailed his mother. 'What's come over you at all?'

'Eh!' he said, looking from one to the other wildly. 'I'm very sorry. Excuse me. I've been talking nonsense. I got irritated. It's this murder in the house and the police asking questions. Then Mr. Corish . . .'

'I'll come over with you and help you to pack,' said his mother. 'You must leave that house at once.'

'No, no,' he said. 'I must go now. I have an appointment.'

'You can't go,' said Agnes. 'Let me get you a cup of tea.'

'I must go,' he repeated.

'O God have mercy on me,' said Mrs. Ferriter. 'Why have you sent me all these trials? Now he's lost his job. Go at once to your Aunt Mary and ask her to speak to Mr. Corish.'

'Yes, yes,' said Ferriter excitedly. 'I'm going there. Good-bye. I'll call in again.'

He dashed for the door.

'Don't let him go,' said Agnes, speaking to her husband.

'Don't try to stop me,' shouted Ferriter to the professor. 'I am unclean.'

He halted as he was going out of the door, looked back and then said in a strange tone:

'That's true. I am unclean.'

HALF an hour later, Ferriter entered the office of the *Catholic Vanguard* in Fleet Street. This office comprised two rooms on the second floor of an old building. In the front room he found a very thin young man and a girl in spectacles, working at a table.

'May I see Father Moran?' he said to the young man.

'He's busy at the moment,' said the young man.

'Ask him whether I can see him,' said Ferriter. 'It's important. You know my name.'

The young man, astonished by Ferriter's distraught expression, glanced at the girl and then knocked at the door leading to the inner room. The girl stared at Ferriter, but she dropped her eyes quickly when Ferriter turned towards her, in his survey of the room. He was deadly pale and he could not keep still. As he was getting on a bus at Rathmines Library, he had seen the tiny man standing in front of the Town Hall across the road.

'He said you may go in,' said the young man, coming out of the inner room.

Ferriter nodded. He passed into the other room and closed the door behind him. Father Moran, editor of the *Catholic Vanguard*, was sitting at a desk, writing rapidly. He did not stand up or raise his head when Ferriter entered, merely waving his hand. Ferriter watched him. After a minute or so the priest laid down his pen and said:

'That's that. Won't you sit down? Throw those papers off that chair. There's no room here. Everything gets cluttered up.'

He was a very plump young man of thirty-six, with red hair and a slightly freckled face, exceedingly short in stature. All his features were correspondingly small, except his ears, which looked a great deal too large for him. He had a shrewd face, which did not inspire confidence. His eyes kept wandering hither and thither jerkily, never resting on any one object for more than a few seconds at a time. His head was birdlike. He kept jerking his shoulders, twitching his nose and moving his rump about on the chair.

'You look ill, he said. 'I don't feel well myself. It's a heavy day. Good Lord! Are we going to get no summer? It's the same everywhere though. I was talking to a friend of mine who has just come back from the south of France. It's terrible there too. I like your article on Round Towers.'

'Have you heard about the murder this morning?' said Ferriter.

'Which murder? Was there a murder? I mean a new one?'

'A woman called Mrs. Boulter who lived in the house where I live was murdered last night,' said Ferriter in a halting voice. 'I came to talk to you about it, as I am concerned in the murder.'

'Gracious me!' said the priest.

He looked at Ferriter with wide open eyes and stuck the end of his fountain pen between his tiny lips. Very hurriedly, Ferriter recited the story, as he had told it to Mr. Corish. While he spoke, the little priest kept looking at him in a curious fashion, furrowing his forehead, blinking and chewing spasmodically at the end of his fountain pen.

'Let me see,' he said, when Ferriter had finished. 'It's a scandalous state of affairs. Mr. O'Leary's son too. It's going to be rather a blow for him if his son was really responsible. Dear me! Of course, in the first place, it would have been rather difficult for the committee to have done anything in the case of a woman like that.

You can't employ them. They're so unreliable. My own opinion is that there must be some sort of prison reform, a kind of better class reformatory for women of that sort. Put them to work. Then again, you are up against the manufacturers, who naturally don't want any sort of government competition. The law is very backward on this whole question. I've a good mind to get the while thing written up in the *Vanguard*.

He was an ambitious little man, who edited the *Catholic Vanguard* for purely personal motives, in order to push himself along towards the high places of the church. Of very acute intelligence, he had made cunning use of current fanaticism, so that he succeeded in making his periodical talked about, owing to its violence of opinion, principally on the question of immoral literature, sexual immorality, Freemasonry and the 'Protestant oligarchy.' This latter organization especially was supposed to be working for the destruction of Ireland as a Catholic country. Even at his early age, his advancement was already secure. He was neck and shoulders above his rivals in the diocese, in cunning, in drawing-room manners and information. He had been to Rome, where he had been favourably received by the Pope. It was common knowledge that he was marked for a bishopric as soon as there was a vacancy. Whether or not he believed in God or in the infallibility of the Pope I cannot say; but I am certain that he despised the mass of people whose violence of opinion he encouraged in the various onslaughts that have recently been made on freedom of thought and conduct. Furthermore, he had a great influence on zealous young Catholic men of Ferriter's type, these latter regarding him as a sort of clerical Mussolini. Ferriter, in particular, had been drawn into the activist movement through Father Moran's propaganda; although he had grown a little suspicious of his leader during recent months, since he had decided to make the sacrifice of blood.

'I asked Mr. Corish to tackle the thing in the *Morning Star*,' said Ferriter, 'but he refused. I had a . . . I had a scheme prepared. Perhaps the *Vanguard* would be better.'

'A scheme?' said Father Moran. 'How do you mean?'

'I regard this murder as an act of God,' said Ferriter excitedly. 'It may indeed be the sign under which . . . behind which . . . it may be the great opportunity that we're seeking for . . .'

He broke down under the glance of the little

priest's darting eyes. Even while he spoke, he told himself that this priest also was an alien, a being of another order of thought, chained to the earth, a tool of society.

'I don't quite catch what you mean,' said the priest. 'How could a murder be an act of God? I take it you mean in the religious sense.'

'Yes,' said Ferriter in a lame fashion. 'I meant it in a religious sense.'

He paused and then continued hurriedly:

'I see a connection between this and the destruction of Sodom and Gomorrah.'

'What's that?' cried Father Moran in astonishment.

Ferriter leaned forward, rubbed his forehead, and said appealingly:

'Please understand me. I foresaw that this was going to happen. Men who are well known and respected in the city, other than Dr. O'Leary, who is after all merely a common libertine, other and important men were using this woman in a bestial fashion, and when I complained to the committee they tried to hush the matter up, simply because they are all in league with sin. For that reason I am convinced that a clean sweep must be made, as in the case of Sodom. Something violent must be done to bring home the horror of the situation to everybody. Don't you think I am right in believing that?'

The little priest sucked the end of the fountain pen far into his mouth. Then he took it away, wiped it on his sleeve and said:

'I'm afraid I don't understand you at all. I'm afraid, in fact, that you are rushing to extremes. The thing to be avoided, you see . . . as a layman, of course, you could not be expected to understand this. But in any case, scandal must be avoided. That would be merely mud-raking, and when mud is stirred up it sticks to everybody. It merely fouls the landscape, so to speak. In a way, the committee were quite right. What should be done, of course, is to get some legislation passed to save unfortunate women from the necessity . . .'

'Please understand me, father,' cried Ferriter, in an agonized voice. 'You don't realize what this means to me. You can't realize it.'

'Well?'

Ferriter clenched his teeth and his fists. He tried to speak and failed. Then after another effort he blurted out:

'I want to ask you something.'

'You may do so,' said the priest almost in a bored tone.

'Do you think that the man who killed this woman is a murderer?'

'Naturally,' said the priest at once. 'As far as I know of the case he obviously must be. She was stabbed in the back, so it cannot have been done in self-defence. It was a particularly foul murder.'

'But if the motives that inspired the man were something different?'

'You mean?'

'If he did it because he wished to . . .'

He paused, looked the priest closely in the face and added fiercely:

'Do *you* also think that prostitutes are a social convenience?'

'Now what on earth are you talking about?'

'I mean this,' cried Ferriter, getting to his feet. 'Here are two people, a man and a woman. The man, already corrupt, takes the woman and makes her corrupt like himself. I have seen her photograph, when she was a young girl, pure as a lily, a Child of Mary, glorious in her beauty. He took this flower and crushed it, made it unclean and foul with sin. Then she in turn preys on human souls, dragging them down. She becomes a harpy preying on the innocent. Do you call it murder to strike her down? Do you think that the man who crushed her should not be hanged?'

The priest leaned back in his chair and said:

'When laymen begin to meddle with theological questions they are sure to get muddled. You should leave these deep problems to more trained minds. What is the Church for, if not for that? If I were you I should avoid meddling with things that are beyond you. . . .'

'Stop,' cried Ferriter in a loud voice. 'Say no more.'

His chest heaved.

'Shall I tell you what you are?' he whispered tensely. 'Just now I see you in your true colours. I shall tell you, in one word: Hypocrite.'

He moved towards the door, turned his head and called back:

'You are a hypocrite and an atheist. I know it now. Where have you led me?'

He hurried out of the room and kept mumbling to himself as he went down the stairs:

'Such are the people that have led me. Where have they led me? O God! Where have they led me?'

Sustained by his fit of anger, he walked rapidly down Fleet Street into Westmorland Street and then across the road, without caring where he went or what happened to him; but on reaching the far side of the street, he paused uncertainly. Where was he to go now?

'Good God!' he said half aloud. 'I have lost my job. Why did I do that? Yes. I'll put an end to it all. I'll commit suicide. They don't care. Nobody cares.'

In answer to this thought, and acting in direct opposition to it, he jumped on a tramcar that was going towards Donnybrook. He dismounted in Fitzwilliam Street and hurried to his aunt's house. This aunt, a sister of his father, was the most important personage connected with the family, as the fortunes of revolution had turned her husband into a Cabinet Minister and she was prominent in government society. Indeed, when he arrived he found that she was having a large tea party in her drawing-room. The servant looked at him with reserve and asked him to wait in a small room, while she announced his presence to his aunt. This reserve on the part of the servant was due to a scene which Ferriter had made on his last visit, when he had called to ask his aunt for help, to procure a job for Teresa.

After he had waited nearly ten minutes the aunt appeared. She was a blowsy woman of fifty, of great size and extremely fat. She resembled those innkeeping women that have gone out of fashion in this country, but may be still seen in France, red of countenance, genially vulgar and continually talking with the voice and arrogance of a sergeant-major. Her face gave the impression that she was always puffing out her cheeks. Her whole body shook when she moved. Her husband, as well as everybody else, was terrified of her; as well he might be, for it was to her, rather than to his feeble talents, that he owed his success.

'Sorry to disturb you, Aunt Mary,' said Ferriter insolently, 'but I am in great trouble.'

'What do you want now?' she said roughly. 'I hope you're more sober in mind than you were last time you came here. Nobody ever comes to see me unless they want something. I believe you're making no great shakes at that job I got for ye. I was talking to Paddy Corish the other day and he said ye were doing very poorly.'

'I have lost my job,' said Ferriter.

'Arrah! What's that ye're saying?' she said. 'Ye've lost yer job. And I suppose ye've come here to ask me to get another one for ye. Faith then if ye go on the way ye are, it's in the poorhouse ye'll pull up, like an old horse going to the knackers. Look at the way ye're dressed, man. How d'ye expect to get on if ye turn yourself out that way? I've seen ye wearing that same old tweed suit as long as I can remember. If ye were dressed properly I could bring ye in and introduce ye to people that might be useful to ye. What are ye going to do now?'

'Very probably I'm going to do something that will create a sensation,' said Ferriter in an impudent tone.

'Oh well!' she said in an absent manner. 'I have no time now to listen to yer schemes. It's probably some other foolish thing ye're after, same as that old strap ye were trying to put on her feet. Why must ye waste yer time with things that don't concern ye? Ye're old enough now to be thinking of getting married and settling down and having a nice, respectable position for yerself, same as the rest of the family. Ye're the only one of them that turned out useless. Start with a little and it won't be long mounting up. Even a single saving certificate. It's a beginning any-way. That's the way everything starts. Hold on. For yer poor father's sake, Lord have mercy on him, I won't hold it against you the ugly way you turned on me last time you were here. I'll do what I can, but I have no time now. I hear some talk of a new paper being started. If there's anything in it, I'll put in a good word for ye, but ye must make an effort to look smarter. I said the same thing to your sister Agnes's husband. He should make himself look tidier and go around more. And he should give less of his lip about things that don't concern him. She's nearly as bad. Sneering at religion never pays. Take my word for it. I must go now.'

'One moment, Aunt Mary,' said Ferriter, drawing himself up to his full height. 'I wonder whether you'd be so anxious to go back to your guests if I told you the truth about what is going to happen, or about what has happened?'

'What are you talking about?' she said coarsely. 'I declare to God I often thought you were a bit touched, but now I'm inclined to be certain of it. You're going to be impertinent again. I can see it in your face. You took after your mother's people. But God forgive me, I don't like to see you going around with a hungry look on your face. Can ye translate a book into Irish? I hear they're looking for good translators.'

Suddenly Ferriter burst out laughing. It was a dry and ugly laugh, like that of a maniac. He showed his teeth and his face creased, as if he were laughing. Yet his eyes stared fixedly, showing no gleam of merriment.

'You are ashamed to introduce me to your guests,' he jeered, 'because I'm shabby and a failure. But in a few hours you can no longer hide me from your guests or from anybody else. They'll all know. Don't you think that will be worse? But at least I shall have my revenge. In a few hours more.'

With that he left the house.

'Mad,' said his aunt, staring after him.

Then she shrugged her shoulders and returned to her guests.

'Back, back,' muttered Ferriter to himself as he hurried down the street. 'Whatever is left exists there. I must go and find it. I am now standing at the door and at any minute I'll enter into the secret. Does God exist and has man got a divine destiny? It's down there in that house where she stooped and I plunged it into her back. Outside of that house there is nothing. All aliens.'

Again he caught a glimpse of the tiny man, standing in the doorway of a tobacconist's shop and immediately he heard voices in his ears, as if devils were shouting insults at him; but his face was now contracted and he was shrinking within the shelter of despair, and he paid no heed to the little man.

'How beautiful it was,' he thought, 'when I

took her to mass and we knelt side by side in the church! Her face looked innocent as in the photograph. Tears were streaming down her cheek and as she was bowed that way, striking her breast, I saw the little curly rows of golden hair on the back of her neck. How happy I was thinking I had saved her! Then he came back and the devil re-entered her.'

He halted in the street and stared in wonder. 'Did I really love her?' he muttered. 'My God! Did I do it through jealousy?'

CHAPTER XI

WHEN he turned into Lower Gardiner Street from Beresford Place, he found a large crowd of curious people staring at the house from the far pavement. In front of the door, a Ford motor car had just come to a halt and a woman was being helped out by the driver. The car was very old and tattered, so caked in dry mud that some urchin had been able to write his name on the back with his finger. The woman was extremely big and unsteady, so that the young man was unable to get her out of the door. Ferriter, in passing, paused to give him assistance, by holding the door open. When she finally got out on to the pavement, she was so exhausted by the effort that Ferriter had to hold her up.

'Pooh! You devil,' she gasped. 'The insides are shaken out o' me. Ugh! The shakin' I got in that rattletrap.'

'Ah! sure,' said the driver, wiping his face with his cap, 'it's not a bad car at all now, and we after makin' that distance in five hours. It must be every inch of . . .'

'Shut your gob,' said the woman fiercely, 'and let me draw breath.'

She was about sixty-five years of age and of enormous girth. Her hair had once been golden, for there were still yellowish streaks in its whiteness, making it look dirty. Her expression was very fierce, as she had powerful tufts of hair sticking out from the centre of her eyebrows, and huge gullets, like a turkey, beginning at her chin and ending away down at the base of her neck, wobbling when she moved her head. Other tufts of hair grew in the deep crevices which age and fat had made in her face. Even on her coarse, fat hands there were hairs as strong as on a man's hand. This hairiness was responsible for her nickname of 'Hairy Maggie Considine.' She wore a small, round, black hat, perched on the topmost coil of her hair. It was very bruised, and a long feather, broken in the middle by the bumping of the car, stuck up at the back of it. A long blue jacket reached nearly to her knees, drawn in very tightly below her ponderous breasts and then coming out over her stomach and haunches in a great balloon. Her skirt trailed on the ground behind her and it was adorned with two flounces of black velvet, one below the knees and one at the bottom. She carried a heavy stick.

'Ah! God bless my sowl!' she cried in a fierce and melancholy voice, as she looked up at the house. 'An' is this where they done her in? My poor darlin' Teresa! The curse o' God on them. Johnny, take that ould car to a garage and get them to do something to it, or I won't travel another yard in it. Go on now. You have no more brains than a badger. Sure it's out of my mind I was when I took you with me, you and your monument of scrap iron. Give us a hand up these steps, sonny.'

Ferriter helped her up the steps, glancing at her furtively and trembling; awed by her mention of Teresa's name. A policeman opened the door and said in a cross tone:

'What do ye want?'

'Faith, then, I want nothing off you, you big good-for-nothing lump,' said the old woman angrily. 'Is it now ye're mounting guard when she's lying stiff over in the morgue? I'm her aunt, Mrs. Considine.'

'Come on in,' he said. 'Hold on a minute. Who are you?'

'I live here,' said Ferriter. 'My name is Ferriter.'

'Oh! Is that who ye are?' said the policeman, looking at Ferriter sharply.

'Who's here in charge?' said Mrs. Considine. 'Is it you?'

'It's me,' said the policeman.

'Well! I've come for her things. God rest yer soul, alannah. It's a sick load to be carrying west with me.'

'I have no orders about that,' said the policeman. 'You'll have to wait here a little while. The chief superintendent'll be here shortly.'

'He said he'd be here now,' said Mrs. Considine.

Ferriter started at the mention of the chief superintendent. The policeman looked at him and said:

'Will you wait here, too, Mr. Ferriter, with this woman? I think, maybe, he'll want to see you, too.'

'But where is he?' cried Mrs. Considine aggressively. 'Ye can't keep me waiting from pillar to post.'

'Now be peaceful, ma'am,' said the policeman. 'Aren't we trying to do our best? Would ye be obliging and come in here?'

He ushered Mrs. Considine and Ferriter into the hall sitting-room, where the dagger had hung.

'May I wait in my room?' said Ferriter timidly. He was awed by meeting her aunt, and he didn't want to be left alone in that room with her.

'No,' said the policeman, looking at him close-ly. 'You better wait here.'

Ferriter went very pale. He knew they were searching his room. He sat down in the chair, where the superintendent had examined him that morning.

'Where is the good woman that looks after the house?' said Mrs. Considine.

'You mean Mrs. Kelly?' said the policeman.

'That's her. She sent me the telegram,' said Mrs. Considine. 'Would ye send her to me, like a good man?'

'I'll go and see,' said the policeman.

He closed the door after him. The old woman floundered to a chair and sat down, gasping and moaning. Ferriter kept glancing at her and then at the door that led into the other room.

'Was it here she lived?' said the old woman in an awed tone.

'Yes. She lived here,' said Ferriter without looking at her.

'And did you know her, asthore?'

'I knew her a little,' he whispered.

'Ah! And would ye tell me what she was like?' said the old woman plaintively. 'How did she look?'

Ferriter felt terribly ashamed, so that he blushed deeply and a flood of tears welled into his eyes and he said in a broken voice, with his eyes on the floor:

'She was very beautiful.'

'Ah! Then I believe you,' said the aunt, 'for she was always beautiful as the dawn in summer. But what good was it to her, only a misfortune? Answer me that, you that look so modest and kindly. Sure there's no use in hiding anything now. Only to speak well of the dead and to pity their transgressions. But she was drove into it. I can tell ye that. Or maybe ye know it yourself. Were ye often in conversation with her?'

'I knew something of her life,' said Ferriter excitedly. 'I know that she was ruined by a certain man and I know the man. I pity her. Oh! Yes, as I hope to see God, I pity her from the bottom of me heart.'

He said this with such fervour that the old woman looked at him with great interest.

'You're a good man,' she said. 'You have an honest nature. If men were all like you, it's not on a journey like this I'd be coming.'

'Do you really mean that?' cried Ferriter. 'Do you think I'm a good man?'

'I seldom go wrong,' she said.

For the first time he raised his eyes to hers. In spite of her ferocious character, she was appalled by the expression of his eyes, so that she drew back in her chair. Then she seemed to brush aside the thought of him, as something useless and alien. She began to talk rapidly.

'I know the man ye mean,' she said. 'Sure she came down to Galway that time she got into trouble. But I could do nothing for her. God help her! She was by that time beyond helping. And she ran away again.'

'Please tell me,' said Ferriter. 'I would like to know very much, what she was like then. I saw a photograph of her in her room. That room in there . . . where she was killed.'

'Was she killed there?'

'Yes.'

'In there?'

'She was killed there,' he gasped and then continued in an excited tone:

'But won't you tell me, because . . . because I tried to take her away from this life, but I failed.'

'Musha, God bless you, asthore. Faith then I'll tell you, for it's good to talk to you and you so good-natured and mild. It's how she was my sister's child, my youngest sister Mary, who worked for Sir George Bodkin of Killuragh

Castle. A rip he was that got eight women into trouble, God forgive him, and Mary was the last of them. He was as old as I am at the time. He married her to his under-gardener and when he himself died, he left them five hundred pounds to bring up the infant. They opened an hotel and then Burke died. Teresa was about five at the time. Mary was well over forty and then she put her foot in it by marrying a poxy peeler. She's dead now, and God forgive me for speaking bad of the dead, but it was fitter for her to start saving her soul than fiddle under the blankets with a bodach like that and he a stranger from the County Mayo. Now look at the result of it. She and her child are dead an' gone, the one with a broken heart, although they say it was cancer of the stomach, the other stabbed in the back by a heathen hyena, while that bould criminal Finnerty is going up for the County Council at the next election. God's curse on the country that hasn't a gunman in it to put a streak o' lead in through his cowardly guts. She had two children with him, two miserable creatures that have been whinging and delicate since they were born, and now the whole place belongs to them. He owns half Killuragh and soon he'll own the rest of it, grabbing all round

him, like a thieving boy in an orchard. He's
brought all his poor relations in after him from the
County Mayo. They began to arrive at his heels,
every one of them as lean and hungry as himself,
and he never stopped till he ousted the poor,
unfortunate girl out of everything. It was
shocking the way he did it. He worried my sister
Mary until she finally signed the document,
handing him over all the property, leaving only
five hundred pounds for Teresa when she was
twenty-one. Says he to Mary: "That's what
Sir George Bodkin left her and how could she
want more?" The scurvy mongrel casting in
her face that the child was a half bastard. But
it wasn't within thousands of pounds of what
was her just share. Although he widened the
business, Mary was doing well herself before he
came. Wasn't it the principal hotel in the western
part of the county, with the gentry from England
coming to fish there? Ye might have heard of
it. It's going yet. The Atlantic Hotel of Killuragh. She made a pile in it, and it was out of
that money he was able to widen out and take
shops and land and trawlers and the rest of it.
If she had a penny she must have had . . .'

Apparently forgetting all about Teresa and the
murder, the old woman began excitedly to

enumerate the values of various properties in Killuragh, going into such details that even pennies became important. Ferriter was becoming very agitated and he finally interrupted her by saying:

'But could you tell me about the convent?'

'Ah! Yes, a mhac,' said the old woman. 'It was a dodge to send her to the convent and get her out of the way. What did she want with a convent? And little good it did her either. They get high notions in them convents.'

'But what was she like in the convent? I have seen her photograph when she was at the convent.'

Instinctively he hid the foot, against which the photograph was concealed, under his chair.

'Indeed she was a simple and innocent girl,' said Mrs. Considine. 'As sweet tempered as a new born lamb. It was only when she went to that hospital that she changed. He wanted to get her out of the way and when her mother died, he having the document signed, he fired her out and sent her to Dublin. And there she met the blackguard that ruined her. She came down to me when she was three months gone. I have a public-house and grocery in Galway. If ye're ever down that way step in and ye'll

178

be welcome. My husband, God rest his soul, started in the cattle trade. A good jobber he was, too. We did our best for her.'

Here she lowered her voice and recounted, with extraordinary coarseness, the means by which she tried to procure an abortion for Teresa, with the assistance of a wise woman from Connemara. They placed her in a barrel of hot water and gave her gin to drink.

'But God's curse on it, whatever herbs were mixed in the potion did no good at all, nor did the baths, nor the gin; only she turned into a sour sort of a drunkard and then bolted.'

Just then the door opened and Mrs. Kelly entered furtively, crossing herself.

'Is this Mrs. Considine?' she said.

The two women shook hands and began to talk rapidly in a low voice about the tragedy. Then Mrs. Kelly turned on Ferriter and said harshly:

'Are you satisfied now?'

Ferriter jumped to his feet and cried out:

'Mrs. Kelly, I want to beg your pardon and yours too, Mrs. Considine. I was unjust to your niece. Will you forgive me?'

'Arrah! What's this?' said Mrs. Considine.

'God above knows!' said Mrs. Kelly. 'Whatever

you have on your soul, Mr. Ferriter, it's not from me you should ask forgiveness.'

'But not for that,' cried Ferriter. 'For the other things. You were kind to me and I was too proud. I felt lonely and ashamed. It was for no other reason. And perhaps it was the same as far as your niece was concerned, Mrs. Considine. I don't know. I only want to say I apologize. I can do no more, as I have nothing to give. If I had I'd give it.'

They stared at him suspiciously. Then he sat down and covered his face with his hands. The women watched him. Suddenly he rose again to his feet, looked at them strangely and hurried out of the room. The policeman was talking to somebody at the door, so Ferriter slipped up the stairs to the bathroom unnoticed. In his hurry, however, he stumbled going in the bathroom door and hurtled across the room, striking the door of the lavatory at the far end with a loud crash. This attracted the policeman's attention. He looked up, caught sight of Ferriter disappearing hurriedly into the lavatory and ran towards the stairs. Ferriter locked the lavatory door, stooped and took the photograph from inside his sock. He looked at it for a moment longingly. Then he bent down and kissed the face. He sighed deeply, tore it into four parts and threw them in the basin. He heard steps outside and pulled the chain quickly. He had meant to tear up the manuscript in the same manner, but already the policeman was knocking at the door. He put his hands to his mouth and blew on the palm that was nearest to his lips.

'Who's that?' he called out.

'Who's in there?' cried the policeman.

Ferriter did not answer for a moment. He was trying to decide whether he should tear up the manuscript and flush it through the pipe. Would they suspect and search? He made a grimace of disgust, unlocked the door, threw it open, faced the policeman and cried out angrily:

'How dare you follow me like that?'

'None of that, now,' said the policeman. 'I'm on guard here. I'm obeying orders.'

'I don't care what you are,' shouted Ferriter. 'You are very impertinent and ignorant. I'm going to report you and get you sacked. What's your number?'

The policeman got furious.

'Come out here,' he said, shifting his belt. 'I'll give you what you're looking for.'

He caught Ferriter roughly by the shoulder and rushed him out through the bathroom, on to the landing. Ferriter, unable to do anything else, turned his head and spat into the policeman's face. Then he ran up the stairs as fast as he could, followed by the guard, who had drawn his baton. On the third flight he passed Miss Beamish, the girl who had discovered the corpse. She was coming down, accompanied by another girl, carrying all her kit. She was about to leave the house, owing to the fright she had got. She leaned against the wall and put her hand to her heart as Ferriter dashed past her. The other girl, turning to quieten her, barred the policeman's way for a few seconds, so that Ferriter reached his room without being caught by his pursuer. He pushed open the door and came face to face with Mr. Lavan, who had just finished searching the room with the assistance of two detectives. Lavan looked at him coolly.

'What's the meaning of this?' cried Ferriter in an angry tone. 'All my things turned inside out. Who gave you leave to come here?'

Lavan calmly walked over to the little table in the centre of the room, picked up a pair of kid gloves and held them out.

'When did you cut yourself?' he said. 'There's blood on these gloves.'

Ferriter stared at the gloves. For a moment,

he was afraid that he was going to fall down in a faint; but the reaction to a mood of defiance was instantaneous. He knew that he was now struggling for his life and the terrible reality of being arrested for murder, with bloody evidence against him, her blood on his gloves, put the affair in an entirely different light from what it had appeared, when he was teasing his aunt about what would happen in a few hours' time. Then, in the rage of humiliation, it did not seem to matter if he were arraigned in court, condemned and hanged. Now, the threat of the noose curdled his blood.

'This is more of your cleverness,' he sneered. 'Blood indeed! That's very clever of you.'

Lavan turned to the policeman, who was now standing awkwardly in the doorway.

'What do you want?'

'He ran up,' said the policeman.

'Either that or he walked up,' said Lavan irritably. 'He can hardly have crawled up, or you might have caught him.'

'I couldn't help it, sir,' grumbled the policeman.

'You have no right to be here,' cried Ferriter defiantly to Lavan, 'or to treat me like this, following me all over the city. Why don't you arrest me and be done with it, if you suspect something? What's behind this plot?'

'One moment, sir,' said the policeman.

Lavan went out on the landing.

'He bolted out of the sitting room, while I was having a word with Tyson at the door,' said the policeman. 'He ran into the lavatory and he had just pulled the chain when I got to him. I think he was doing away with something.'

'Get back to your post,' said Lavan, 'and keep your wits about you.'

He returned to Ferriter after closing the door.

'Now, Mr. Ferriter,' he said brusquely, 'do you feel like telling me how this blood got on your gloves?'

Ferriter looked hopelessly around the room, as if seeking a means of escape. The bed had not been made. Evidently nobody had come into the room since he had left it that morning. Even the tea tray, with a used teacup, lay on the table.

'How odd!' he thought.. 'I drank from that cup before I went downstairs.'

He did not answer Lavan's question, but walked slowly over to the bed and sat down on it.

'Is there anything else you have found that interests you?' he said.

'Just a cigarette,' said Lavan.

'A cigarette?'

'Yes. Apparently the one you borrowed from Fitzgerald. You must have forgotten to smoke it. Of course, you smoke very rarely.'

'Your sarcasm is very stupid,' said Ferriter insolently. 'But what could one expect from a policeman?'

Lavan flushed, and he had to bite his lip to prevent himself from losing his temper.

'Do you generally keep your gloves in your dressing gown?' he said, after a pause.

'I don't see any reason why I should tell you where I keep my gloves,' said Ferriter.

'You're not particularly interested in your gloves,' said Lavan.

'Not very.'

'Then you won't mind my taking them with me.'

'Certainly I do. They are my property.'

'So? Then, perhaps I'll have to take you as well.'

Ferriter stared at him menacingly. He wanted to blubber now, but still he could not resist the desire to be impertinent – like a naughty child, who is sure of a whipping and wants to get full value for his misdeed. At that moment, he felt sure that all was lost.

'Come, now,' said Lavan, in a confidential tone. 'What's the use of adopting that attitude? Won't you be reasonable? Why blame me? I'm only doing my duty. It's no use your pretending to be offended by my searching your room, because I have a warrant to do so and . . .'

Suddenly Ferriter held out his hand and interrupted him.

'Hold on,' he said. 'I'm really not offended by your presence here. You can do what you please with the gloves and with the cigarette too. It was something else that offended me; rather many things that have happened to me in the course of this day. It's all so trivial, this melodrama of bloody gloves and an unsmoked cigarette. Perhaps I am wrong: that I have been wrong all the time. I'm not sure yet. When I am sure, I give you my word that everything will be laid bare. Do you understand?'

Lavan shook his head. He pulled his hat a little farther down on his forehead, so that it shielded his eyes. He stared intently at Ferriter; but the latter had now completely recovered his self-possession. Growing despair more strongly fortified him, as he withdrew all the outposts of his strength towards the centre where his mind was struggling to defend the last belief.

'I see,' said Ferriter. 'You insist on being the policeman and nothing more. Trying to hypnotize me. That is on a par with the gloves and the cigarette. My dear man, it's not there you should search for evidence of the crime. I gave you what evidence I could against one man who was responsible, the one you have now in custody.'

'Don't fool yourself,' said Lavan. 'He's not now in custody. He has been bailed out, and the charge against him has nothing to do with this murder.'

'Indeed!' said Ferriter. 'He no longer interests me. I have gone beyond that now. You have not got enough jails to house the multitude of people whom I now recognize to be responsible.'

'Enough of that rubbish, Ferriter,' said Lavan irritably. 'Let's get back to realities. I've heard all that stuff from you this morning. Have you any explanation to offer me as to how blood got on these gloves?'

'None at this moment,' said Ferriter. 'Have you an explanation yourself?'

'Yes,' said Lavan. 'I think I have it pieced together pretty well now.'

'What have you pieced together?'

'Do I have to tell you?'

'If it amuses you.'

'For the last time I ask you to tell me how this blood got on your gloves.'

'You are forgetting the cigarette,' said Ferriter mockingly. 'Why not put the two together? Listen.' He got to his feet and came closer to Lavan. 'You are about to charge me with the murder of Teresa Burke, commonly known as Mrs. Boulter, on the evidence of finding in my room a pair of bloody gloves and an unsmoked cigarette. Is not that so?'

The two men stared at one another in silence for several moments. So tense had the situation become that neither of them was aware of the presence of the detectives, who stood in the background, astonished by this strange scene and a trifle terrified by Ferriter. Although the man was outwardly frail and timid of body, his face a deadly pallor, except for two bright red patches on his cheeks and his legs swayed beneath the weight of his slight frame, the abnormal condition of his mind gave forth gigantic power.

'You won't answer me?' he cried. 'Have you changed your mind? Just now you were certain. What has made you change? You're no longer confident. You are wise.'

At last Lavan found tongue:

'Hold on,' he said. 'Who told you I had

changed my mind? If you insist, I definitely . . .'

'Don't,' said Ferriter hurriedly, holding up his hand and taking a pace to his rear. 'Don't do it. What time is it now?'

One of the detectives looked at his watch and mumbled that it was six o'clock.

'Six o'clock,' said Ferriter. 'Let me see. Will you give me five hours? At eleven o'clock I'll come to you. Make it later. This happened at two. Let me come to you at two. Then I shall deliver up the real murderer. Is that a bargain?'

Lavan folded his arms on his bosom and looked him up and down. Then he shook his head slowly. Ferriter became very agitated and his head began to quiver. In a quavering voice he said quietly, but very hurriedly:

'If you refuse you'll gain nothing, and you'll do irreparable damage. I have to make a very important investigation before I make a statement. I can't explain to you what it is, because you wouldn't understand. But I may tell you that I have to find out the EXACT identity of the murderer. These gloves that you have found have something to do with it, but it was not the man that wore the gloves that killed her. Do you understand that?'

He raised up his hand and cried in a loud voice:

'It was not the man that wore the gloves that killed her, and if you refuse to grant me this favour you shall never know. Never. You may hang me, but I shan't speak.'

Lavan looked enquiringly at the two detectives. Then he walked towards the door and stood there with his back turned to Ferriter, one hand clasping his elbow, the other rubbing his chin, trying to come to a decision. After a few minutes he came back and said:

'Tell me exactly, Ferriter, what you want?'

'It would be no use telling you,' said Ferriter sadly. 'You wouldn't understand. You would just think I'm mad. Later, that may be so, but in any case, whether I break down or not, if you leave me alone for a few hours, you will have the murderer's confession and you'll have the murderer in your possession.'

'Can't you tell me now who is the murderer?'

'That's what I want to find out and . . . and something else too, much more important for me.'

'What's that?'

'It's no use telling you. You wouldn't understand. What are you afraid of? If you wish you can keep a dozen of your men at my heels. Search me. I have no weapons. I can't escape, for it's not from you or your judgment that I want to escape. I, as I sit here, have only been an accomplice after the act.'

'All right,' said Lavan suddenly.

As soon as he had said this, Ferriter almost leaped forward, clutched his hand, stooped and kissed it before Lavan could stop him. Ferriter was beside himself with joy, so that Lavan's suspicions were renewed. Ferriter noticed this, and hastened to explain the cause of his joy.

'You don't know what I have suffered since this happened,' he cried, 'trying to shield the murderer. And it was only just a little while ago that my eyes were opened, while I was talking to Teresa's aunt, Mrs. Considine. I realized that he was a devil instead of the angel I thought him to be. I admit that I have been under his influence for the past two months. He has used me to cover up his tracks. And there are others beside him, wolves in sheep's clothing. I'll expose them all. They have all been using me.'

'Can't you tell me now? Why must you wait?'

'Not now,' said Ferriter.

Then he added after a pause:

'Not now, because I'm under oath.'

Lavan looked at him for a long time in silence. Then he shrugged his shoulders and said:

'Very well. I'll chance it. How long will it take you to find out . . . whatever you want to find out?'

'I asked you to give me until two o'clock.'

'I'll give you until midnight.'

'I agree.'

'In the meantime I'm keeping you under close observation. Any attempt you make to escape . . .'

'You needn't be afraid.'

Lavan rolled up the gloves carefully in some paper and put them in his pocket.

'You may go now,' he said, 'wherever you want to go.'

Ferriter sat down on the bed.

'I want to stay here a little while,' he said. 'It's too soon yet, to go where I want to go. I want to think.'

'You're quite sure that you're just going to think?'

Ferriter looked at him and then smiled faintly.

'No,' he said. 'You may set your mind at rest on that point. I have never thought of that. I would never do that.'

'Go ahead, then,' said Lavan. 'I expect I'm making a fool of myself.'

Ferriter shook his head and then, becoming weary of argument, he put his elbows on his knees and bowed his head over his crossed hands.

'Come along,' said Lavan.

He left the room, followed by the two detectives. Then, when the door had closed after them, Ferriter raised his head and smiled.

CHAPTER XII

'WHAT is happening now?' he whispered. 'It's all so different from what I had supposed. Already it seems such a long, long time since I felt angry with her. Now I only feel ashamed and I could not raise a finger to molest her if she lived. I could talk to her in quite a different way and look her in the eyes without passion, as with someone very dear to me. Indeed I could look at her with tenderness and tell her everything, and I am certain she would understand. Even this queer thing I have done, she would understand that too. Then what do I fear? If I could humble myself before her now and ask for her forgiveness, why not before the others? That's what is strange. I have done them no wrong and yet I fear them, as if I had sinned against them and not against her. What can they do to me? They can only take what has always been a torture and send me where she has already gone. But where is that? I felt it was here in this house, the solution of the problem and yet I hear nothing.'

He looked around the room, his ears intent.

There was complete silence. Then he smiled again and said:

'It was all futile and a delusion. As if a pointing finger led them towards me, crying "That is the man", they came directly, the hounds of Heaven or of Hell, I know not which. Speak then, Almighty God, before I go to confess this sin and tell me whether it was You or Your eternal enemy that took possession of me. Speak if You live.'

He rose to his feet and stood erect, his hands drawn stiffly like a soldier by his sides. Still there was silence. Then terror such as he had not yet experienced took possession of him; for out of the heavy stillness came a rumbling sound, distant in the firmament, a thunderclap that echoed many times. Was it an answer? He sank down slowly to the bed and hid his face, afraid to listen longer. There was no further sound. The storm had not yet broken in its full; but this one clap was for him a blast upon God's trumpet. Furtively he put down his hands and took the manuscript from his sock. He held it out before him and twisted it about many times. Then he straightened it and read the title. Cautiously he turned over the page and continued to read:

'Antichrist is standing at the gates of Christendom. Already he has taken the field in Russia, in Mexico and in Spain. The temples of God are in flames and His priests are hanging from the gibbets. The vultures of paganism are massed above the red banners of Antichrist, swooping down among the blazing ruins of Christianity to devour and pillage. In every corner of the world, the red missionaries of Antichrist are setting alight the torch of atheism among the ignorant masses, in the garb that the evil demon has always worn, offering the gifts of the Serpent that drove man from paradise — greed and lust. Afar off in the dark lands where the banner of Christ has not yet been unfurled, save for a few scattered preachers of the gospel, who have begun to reap God's harvest among the pagan millions, the march of Christianity has been stayed, and these millions are ready to swear allegiance to the Eternal Enemy.

'How does Christendom stand in face of this menace? Alas! Instead of arming for battle it is wallowing in debauchery almost equal to that of pagan Rome before God's anger struck down that leprous Empire. The riches of this earth have blinded the eyes of true believers, so that they seek not the kingdom of Heaven, but waste in feasting and folly that precious time which has been granted us as a preparation for the life

196

hereafter. Instead of organising for the crusade against the forces of Antichrist, Christendom is holding parley with the Red Terror and even protecting with its bosom the spawn of the poisonous vermin that are going to destroy it. For greed and lust have poisoned Europe, until it rots at the core.

'How then shall we prepare to meet the Eternal Enemy and drive him back annihilated? Let us not trust in armaments or gold, for they are useless unless our hearts are purified. The soldiers of the Lord, if they march with God's blessing, need no more powerful weapon than the jaw-bone of an ass to triumph. But if their souls are stained with inner foulness, and if God in His divine wrath has finally decided that man must be cast off without redemption from the gates of paradise, to be drowned in the deluge of atheistic Communism and handed over to the mercies of the Eternal Enemy, no material force is of avail.

'Fellow soldiers of Christ, we must make another sacrifice of blood. This is necessary, just as the sacrifice of Calvary was necessary, in order to give us a fresh realization of man's purpose on this earth. A violent shock is necessary to show us the horror of our sins, just as the burning of

Sodom and Gomorrah was necessary. The corruption of materialism has even spread into the Church, giving to the State prerogatives that belong to God's representatives. Sin is treated with courtesy and its freedom is merely curtailed in order to permit the smooth functioning of the State machine. But an end must be put to that by a violent expression of the anger of the faithful. Sinners must be struck down in death, so that we may be redeemed by their blood. We must purify ourselves by pouring out the blood of sinners. We must put an end to sin and corruption by this sacrifice. Too long have the just been sacrificed on the altar of Mammon. Now the sacrifice must be the blood of the agents of Antichrist. . . .'

Suddenly he dropped the manuscript to the floor and shuddered. He drew his hands slowly over his face and sighed. He had not understood the words that he had read. They had lost their meaning. His mind had not listened to them. It was occupied by the thought of Teresa and by the fear which the thunderclap had caused.

'Now it is clear to me,' he muttered, 'that I must look for no help from this document. I wrote it afterwards. First I decided to kill her and then I wrote it. It is but a written formula of excuse. It wasn't even out of my own head, but windy rubbish from the others.'

Then he cried out angrily, almost in tears with chagrin:

'They did not dare, but they told me and I dared. Then they turn their backs on me.'

He began to laugh hysterically. But he presently checked himself and said, as if soothing a child:

'Hush, hush! Perhaps all is not lost yet. I shall confess and then like the flowing of sweet, sunlit water the grace of God shall fall on me and I'll be at peace. That's why God has been silent all this long day, because I was full of arrogance and refused to bow down before Him as a murderer. Now I humble myself like the meanest worm and ask His forgiveness. I shall tell Him everything as it really was, how I loved her and then killed her in a frenzy. I'll tell Him I don't feel angry any more with her. If she were here I'd lay my head on her lap, just as if she were my mother or my sister Lily. I could take her hand and we could talk and smile at one another, for I'm sure that she too could understand what beautiful things there are in the world, flowers and sunlit water flowing and the talk of the mountain wind. No, no. On the

199

contrary, perhaps nothing at all is lost, but in fact gained, a great deal is gained, because now, by this act, I am equal to her. What appeared strange and hostile in her is no longer strange and hostile, for she had already travelled this road and gone farther. She had suffered already and was alone, just as I have been this day. What is really beautiful in the human soul is not purity, but the struggle to regain lost purity. All the beautiful virtues are then brought to the front, pity and humility foremost among them. Love such as this is a sweet and gentle thing. There can be no pain, even when I myself am sacrificed, for I shall go singing to the scaffold as to a throne.'

He stood up, folded his arms and smiled. He felt at peace.

'I must go now,' he said. 'I must confess.'

Yet he did not move. A heavy rain had begun to fall. It was very hot and there was no wind. The rain made a loud sound and it fell with great force, thickly, in large drops. He stood motionless for a long time, with his eyes closed, breathing calmly, as if he were falling asleep. Then the rain stopped suddenly, just as if the shower had been the emptying of a large vat in the firmament. He shook himself, took his raincoat from the wardrobe and put it on. He looked at the manuscript which he had thrown on the floor and walked towards it dreamily. Then he shook his head and left the room. After he had closed the door, he leaned against it for a little while. The thought of confession ceased to give him peace as soon as he left the room. He again felt arid within him and afraid of what would happen when midnight came and he had to meet Lavan. When he moved away from the door he felt weak. He gazed longingly at the little kitchen on the landing, knowing that he would never see it again. All these common dead things now seemed to be part of himself. He was being gradually stripped of these things, and soon there would be nothing but his frail body to meet the noose and then eternal silence without movement. Each downward step intensified his illusion of being stripped, and he saw with enlarged eyes the disappearance of doors, stairs, walls, banisters, all friendly and habitual things, although they all had been hateful to him in his arrogance. They were now all transformed and encased in comforting magnificence, like the bleak face of a sheer cliff to a man slipping without foothold to his death.

What silence! A cock crowing at night!

CHAPTER XIII

IT was a little after seven when he arrived at the church. Owing to the storm, which now lashed the earth with a continuous torrent of rain, only a few people had arrived for confession. They were kneeling near the confessional box in the rear. He drew apart, some distance up the church towards the altar, not wishing to take his turn, but to wait until everybody had gone. He took off his dripping raincoat and knelt. He made no effort to commune with God or to prepare for confession, not even making the sign of the cross. What he had to say needed no preparation. In fact, he was afraid to think of what lay concealed in his mind; that load which had caused him such acute pain all day.

As he knelt he could hear the droning of the priest's voice granting absolution. The voice started on a high note and then faded away into a mumble. He found that terrifying. Furthermore, the atmosphere of the church itself was unaccountably hostile. He had been in the habit of visiting it since coming to Lower Gardiner

Street, not only for his religious duties, but also for prayer and meditation at odd moments. Such had been his devotion and his reliance on God for spiritual enjoyment, that he had gone to church in his spare time, as other young men seek women, games, dancing or the theatre. Until now he had always found peace and comfort under its roof. It had been the house of God, its air pregnant with God's spirit, an oasis in the desert of materialism, a place of miracles and sweet music and mercy, where the soul became exalted and the eye of Heaven shone with a clear image of eternal beauty. He had often come thither oppressed by a load of sorrow and he had found comfort in the contemplation of the unfathomable delights belonging to God's mighty kingdom. From the earth's jungle, where he had been defeated in the battle with greedy men for advancement and wealth, he had come for succour into the incensed fortress of the Lord and the Lord had never failed to answer his cry for help. There the burnished glory of the altar had gilded his poverty. His humiliation had found divine companionship in the despised Christ who dragged His cross from Jerusalem to Calvary. He had felt himself a child of God.

Now all was tawdry and alien. The silence was oppressive. He looked at the other penitents with repulsion. They offended him by their breath, by the rain that glittered on their clothes, by the servile expression on their faces. In this, his greatest sorrow and humiliation, God was cut off from him and he was an interloper in the church.

Then he remembered a vision he had once, while at school, of Lucifer's revolt. It was after a grievous humiliation. On Wednesdays and Sundays, when all the boys got into Rugby football kit and played matches, Ferriter and a few others, who were excused games owing to their delicate health or the fixed prejudice of their parents, wandered about in the unmarked portions of the sports ground, kicking a spare ball to keep themselves warm. On this day it was exceedingly cold and Ferriter was the only one of the non-players present. The prefect, a boisterous and good-natured fellow, without much subtlety, insisted on Ferriter playing centre three-quarter on the second fifteen's ground. Ferriter objected strongly, and this angered the prefect, so that he lost his temper and made pretence of whipping the lad with the cincture of his soutane. All the boys were delighted, as they despised Ferriter. They joined with the prefect in humiliating him. By mutual agreement of both teams, the ball invariably came out of the scrum on Ferriter's side. The stand-off half, on receiving the ball, ran up and placed it carefully in Ferriter's hands, to make sure of his holding the pass. Then they all shouted, urging him to run with the ball; but before he could run a yard, the opposing centres, halves and third row forwards were down on him, tackling him with a great show of violence and then forming a loose scrum over him when he fell. After twenty minutes he was so shattered that he had to be helped off the field, amid the jeers of the others. After dinner he made matters worse by complaining of the prefect to the dean of discipline and then reporting to the infirmary for treatment. That evening, all the boys tormented him in the recreation ground, shouting the word 'Dolly,' a nickname given at the school to boys who were not athletic, who aroused the affectionate interest of the masters by their good looks, or who differed from the general herd by an objectionable degree of intelligence and refinement. When he got to bed that night, he prayed hard to God for comfort; but the other boys in the dormitory still kept whispering the hated nickname after the lights had gone out. This filled his heart so much with bitterness that he was unable to evoke God's normal image and he saw Him for the first time as a sour and corpulent old man, jealous of beauty and genius, a partisan of the common, vulgar fellows who jeered. Then a strange thing happened to him; for he, who had always been exemplary in his devotion and in his religious humility, suddenly took sides with Lucifer, whom he imagined, like himself, in revolt against the monstrous idiocy of Heaven. He saw the beautiful archangel, magnificently dressed, anointed with sweet unguents, surrounded by a host of angels almost as beautiful as himself, remonstrating with God and demanding that God should civilize Heaven. But God overwhelmed them with great brutality and cast them into Hell.

Now Ferriter shuddered with pity for the fallen angels, a vast number of whom were killed in their descent. He saw them vividly. Each angel's destruction made him sensible of an acute pain, as if he himself were being strangled in a noose and then cast into a deep pit.

He shuddered violently at the vision of the noose and tried to remember whether he had seen the noose in bed that night at school. Certainly, now, on recalling the vision, he could distinctly see the angels in the noose and he felt its pressure on his own throat. He saw the trap-door sprung and the dark pit, although there was a bandage over his eyes. But then, as a relief from this torment, he heard the escaped angels shouting to him in gratitude. They were making merry in some hidden place, which was loud with their triumphant laughter and their singing. They made him rich promises of pleasure and asked him to hurry towards them through the trap-door and the pit. He joined in their merriment, until he was startled to find somebody tapping him on the shoulder. He looked and saw that a middle-aged woman in the seat behind him was tapping his shoulder with her umbrella.

'What do you mean by giggling in church?' said the woman. 'Are you out of your senses? What is there to laugh at here?'

'I beg your pardon,' he said. 'I . . . I didn't know that I was laughing. I'm very sorry.'

She looked at him severely and said:

'Behave yourself, then.'

Then she snorted and went up the church towards the altar rails, looking back at him in disgust several times. He saw her kneel by the rails and bless her forehead, her bosom and her shoulders with the cross of her rosary beads. He covered his face with his hands, but he did not feel ashamed at having laughed. Neither did he fear the Church or God. He felt angry. The thunder in the firmament was now bursting with great violence and the church had grown dark, made almost lightless by the rain that fell. Yet he felt exhilarated, still hearing the merry voices of the fallen angels who had escaped from God.

As on a wild spring day the curtain of the passing clouds is swept from the sun's face and it shines a little on the windy earth and then again is shuttered, making the gloomy cold more fearsome than before, so when the vision of the escaped angels making merry passed, the murderer returned to God in greater fear. The moment for confession was drawing nearer. Now there was only one other person waiting. Penitents had ceased to enter the church. As he moved back towards the box to take his turn, he tried in great haste to recapture that mood of contrition which had given him consolation in his room; when submission softened his heart and banished arid despair from his bosom. Yet he found that some spirit hostile to God reared its head like a snake within him, defiantly un-believing, making great controversy about the solution of the vital problem.

'Does God exist? Has man got a divine destiny? Do you believe that you can find it in this miserable wooden box? What's going to be revealed? Nothing but your cowardice. Revolt before suffering this last humiliation.'

A penitent came out. The last penitent entered the box. The priest began to mumble. Then that part of him that trembled in fear of God took complete 'possession. He began to pray with great fervour, making a last despairing effort to believe and to receive mercy. Such was the violence of this effort that his very bowels felt pain. But the image of God did not materialize. He was appealing to something vague and non-existent. He began to sob. Tears trickled down his cheeks. His mind became confused and he had no idea what he was going to tell the priest. Instead of God's image, he saw Teresa, with tears rolling down her cheeks in two great streams. She was weeping with him, and her sorrow was as great as his. It seemed also that she was waiting for him to release her and that she was held bound in some hidden place. Then, to his horror, he thought that it

o

was the dagger sticking in her back that held her bound, and he began once more to haul it forth, but it resisted all his efforts, for her body had turned into stone and his arms had become lifeless.

He was so absorbed by this contemplation that he did not notice the departure of the last penitent until the priest opened the door of the box, put out his head and said gruffly:

'Are you waiting for confession?'

'Yes, father.'

Ferriter jumped up hurriedly, walked over and knelt against the grille. The priest closed the door and pulled back the slide from the grille.

'Bless me, father, for I have sinned.'

The priest began to mumble. Ferriter recited the act of contrition.

'How long is it since your last confession?'

'A fortnight, father.'

He could dimly see, through the network of the grille, a stole and a round white collar and a dark body sitting in the gloom of the box. Again he heard the merry fallen angels and a voice said to him that it was futile confessing to God through the priest, but that he should address himself direct to Lucifer, who possessed greater refinement and intelligence than God. That voice unnerved him, so that he could only stammer incoherently in answer to the priest, when asked what sins he had committed since his last confession.

'Speak more distinctly,' said the priest irritably. 'I can't hear you.'

'I want to tell you something very serious, father,' said Ferriter loudly.

'I didn't tell you to shout,' said the priest. 'What is it?'

'I think my last three confessions were bad.'

'What's that? Now you are whispering again. Please remember that I'm very tired. I've had a long and hard day and I've got a headache. Have some consideration.'

'Yes, father. I concealed something in my last three confessions, but then I was not aware that I was contemplating a grievous sin.'

'I don't exactly understand you. How could you conceal it if you were not aware of it?'

'I was aware of it but not as a sin. It appeared to be something else at that time, something glorious, in fact.

'Come, come. Tell me about it. Now please collect yourself and speak distinctly.'

Ferriter opened his mouth to begin, but he heard the priest yawn and paused in confusion.

Again the priest commanded him gruffly to tell his story. Finally he began:

'Some time ago a woman came to live in the house where I have a room. She was with a man whom I understood at that time to be her husband, but who afterwards left her and went to England. The man was not her husband and was living in sin with her. From the moment I saw her, she had a very disturbing effect on me. It was not exactly her beauty that disturbed me, although it was great, but some strange quality in her presence, a quality which had never struck me before in any other woman with whom I had come in contact. That quality appealed to something very violent in my nature. Indeed it was directly responsible for an illness which forced me to spend some time in a nursing home after Christmas. I did not know at the time I was getting ill that she was responsible or that my attitude towards her was anything other than a natural antipathy for her character, but when I was in hospital and I had time to think, lying in bed, I realized that she was the cause of my serious trouble with my health and the growing disgust for my work, my dissatisfaction with life and my morbid attitude towards everything. It all became accentuated after my meeting with her, although I had always been rather delicate and unhappy. But until then I had been able to stick to a rigid discipline of conduct and dieting. Through prayer and various devotions I had been able to control my dissatisfaction.'

'Yes, yes,' said the priest hurriedly, irritated by the detailed manner in which Ferriter was telling his story.

'Even while the man was living with her,' continued Ferriter, 'her conduct had been very bad, but when I came out of hospital it became much worse. It soon became obvious to me that she was a harlot.'

'Dear, dear,' said the priest.

'As the sin of impurity has always been extremely repugnant to me,' said Ferriter with some heat, 'I felt that my hatred of her was justified as the normal attitude of a Christian man. Now I see that it probably, even at that time, had another and quite different origin.'

'Was this the sin you concealed?' said the priest. 'Did you find pleasure in hating her?'

'No, father,' said Ferriter. 'That was not the sin. Neither did I find any pleasure in hating her. It hurt me and kept me awake at night.'

'Thinking of her?'

'Not exactly of her, father, but of the other people associated with her.'

'Were these thoughts improper?'

'Stupid man,' thought Ferriter, in sudden anger, 'why can't he understand?'

'I cannot remember now, father,' he continued, making an effort to feel humble, 'I can only remember their effect on me. I only know that I was continually lapsing into a sort of day dream, imagining conversations with her, arguments in which I forced her to take notice of me and to realize that I was her superior and that I despised her. It was all very confused. I must say that I have always suffered from a feeling that people ignored me unjustly. In society I have never felt at ease, or able to join in the general conversation, so that . . .'

'Continue your story,' interrupted the priest. 'This is all very obscure.'

'One night about two months ago, I came home from work a little after midnight and there were sounds of a quarrel coming from her bedroom. It was not unusual for me to hear noise in her rooms, but it was the first time I had heard a quarrel. I must confess now also that I had often delayed on the stairs, listening to the sounds in her room, so that I could hear her voice. I could not force myself to go upstairs without eavesdropping. Although I pretended to believe that I listened in disgust, or simply through a sense of duty, because I belonged at that time to a vigilance society and it was part of our duty to report cases of immorality, I really listened for personal reasons. I wanted to hear her voice, because it was particularly soft and melodious, and it gave me an intense and passionate pleasure, even though I lay awake at night afterwards, hating it for the pleasure it gave me. This night, however, I heard a man's voice, using foul language and threatening to murder her. I got furious, not with her, but with the man. I decided to interfere. Indeed, there was no time for coming to a decision. Although I have said this morning to somebody else that I hesitated, I don't think that was correct. I was carried away before I knew what I was doing. I knocked at the door and threatened to report them both to the police. The man rushed out: he was a doctor of my acquaintance, and he laid violent hands on me. I went upstairs but I came down soon afterwards to have a bath. I found the woman lying drunk on the bathroom floor. Her mouth was bleeding. She was partly naked, as she wore only a dressing gown which was disordered. As I looked at her, lying there half naked on the floor, I was overcome with desire for her.'

Ferriter uttered this last phrase with great force, and then paused to take in a deep breath. The priest moved on his seat. He had begun to take interest in the narrative. He mumbled something vaguely as to whether the penitent had given way to this desire, but Ferriter continued without paying any attention to the mumbled question.

'I felt both ashamed and angry at the same time as I felt this violent desire. I was angry with her for lying drunk on the floor, with her body exposed, tempting me; angry and ashamed; and yet I took pleasure in her beauty. All that is very distinct, as I have spent weeks brooding over it. It was one of the memories which I cherished in preparing my strength to do what I have done. I wanted to run away and hide from the temptation. Then, however, it appeared to be cowardly to run away and I let pity for her take control of me. I knelt beside her on one knee, took her in my arms and shook her. At first she seemed to be unconscious. She was breathing heavily and her eyes were closed. I leaned her against my bended knee, put my arm around her and rested her head on my bosom. I remember that I felt extraordinarily happy as she lay that way in my arms. I began to rock her as if she were a child. She opened her eyes and looked at me. Her eyes were glazed with drunkenness. Then my pity for her turned into loathing, seeing how hard and callous her eyes were. They were full of sin. I asked her what was the matter. She said nothing, but she dropped her head on my shoulder and went limp. I tried to put her on her feet, but she could not stand. She began to titter. It was horrid. I washed her mouth with my sponge and then I carried her out of the bathroom. That journey down the flight of stairs was a torture to me afterwards, for I kept recalling the sensual pleasure of having her in my arms and I felt angry with myself for not having taken advantage of it at the time, for she made advances to me, while mumbling about the man who had threatened her. I laid her on the bed. Then she recovered with surprising quickness and grew malicious on recognizing me. She kept ordering me to fetch her things and I obeyed, even though she asked me to do unnecessary and foolish things and although I knew that she was making fun of me. At last she took my arm and made me sit on the bed beside her. She still refused to cover herself. Then she became aggressive and tried to fondle me.'

'Indecently?'

'No, father. I shouldn't dwell on this part of my story at all, except that I want to get everything in order. I took away her arm and reasoned with her. But she only laughed and tried to strip herself naked. I prevented her doing so, and then went to the door, intending to leave her, but I returned again to reason with her once more. This time my reasoning took effect and she became sorry for having insulted me. She apologized and then she told me the story of her life, how she had been ruined by this doctor, how she was a prostitute and how he had deserted her child, who was now being reared as a Protestant in a family of Quakers. Her story was so pathetic, and she told it in such a despairing way, that my irritation with her changed into pity and I felt really tender towards her. Then we became very friendly.'

'You mean that you became friendly with her in an improper way?' asked the priest.

Ferriter almost shouted his denial. He was becoming irritated by the vulgar interest which the priest displayed in his story.

'We became friendly in quite a different way,' he continued rather insolently. 'I saw in her, not a prostitute to be loathed, but a human soul like myself, suffering, and in need of help. She gave me to understand that she wanted to be saved from her life of sin, and I promised to help her. All that was very beautiful for me, very wonderful indeed, especially when she shed tears. Indeed, until I got to my room, I felt exalted as I had never felt since my first communion, as if some wonderful miracle were being performed within me. But when I tried to sleep, I kept starting up, disturbed by thoughts of her.'

'Were these thoughts improper?'

'Yes, father,' said Ferriter wearily. 'I imagined situations in which I was intimate with her.'

'Did you give way to these thoughts?'

'Yes. I gave way to them.'

'By act?'

'Please let me continue, father. All this is one act, and I don't want to lose my sense of values by examining pebbles so closely that I fail to see the pyramids. In any case, I confessed all these things already. I am merely dwelling on them so that you may understand everything.'

'Very well, then. I don't want to confuse you.'

'At that time I understood these improper desires were inspired by the devil, in order to terrify me from making an attenpt to save her soul. I understood that the devil tempted me, hoping I might let her sink into the pit, and that it was unfair to blame her for my weak nature.'

'That was correct,' said the priest.

'The caretaker of the house was to my knowledge assisting this woman to lead an immoral life, by letting men enter through the basement door and to leave by the same way, secretly. Next morning the caretaker came into my room and said that the woman wished to see me. I threatened the caretaker that I was going to take very drastic action, unless she stopped turning the house into a brothel. Then I went down to see the woman. She was very sorry for what had happened on the previous night and I am certain that she was really repentant. She looked still more beautiful in this mood. It seemed that the evil of her life had had no effect on her. She looked as fresh and as pure as in the photograph I had seen on her dressing table the night before. That was a photograph taken when she was a young girl. I must say that it had a great effect on me. It was that, I think, more than anything else, which deepened my passion for her and made it noble, giving it that spiritual quality which glorifies ardent affections — makes them sacred. Really, we can only love in that way things that are pure. I now admit this for the first time. I have never before admitted it, not even to myself. I have always been ashamed of anything relating to love for woman. That morning I loved her with a love that was pure and holy. It was then that I noticed for the first time the tiny golden curls that grew at the back of her neck. I saw them when she leaned her head on her arms against the mantelpiece. I then wanted to kneel before her!'

'What's that? You wanted to kneel before her? What do you mean?'

'It was when she agreed to go to mass with me. That convinced me that my love for her was noble and that I would overcome the temptations of the devil. I wanted to bring back her innocence, just as I had seen her in the photograph, when she was a Child of Mary. That is why I wanted to kneel before her. I also wanted to give thanks to God for the heavenly ornament of her beauty. Oh! No. There was nothing at all sacrilegious in my wanting to kneel before her. At that moment I felt that she was united with me in the peace of God. Indeed, for the first time in my life I was really happy. When we were leaving the room to go to mass, she put her arms around my neck and she kissed my cheek. That kiss is another link in the chain of our mutual destruction. It's still sacred to me in spite of the torture it has caused me. Yet, at that moment she had already betrayed me. At least, it afterwards appeared to me, in my anger, as the kiss of Judas. But why should I think so? Why should I blame her for being constant to him? Now I see that it was less through sinfulness than through the generosity of her nature that she went back to him. Even in lust there is virtue, and who is to know on what level was her love for him?'

He shuddered. The priest now had his ear to the grille and he was listening intently. Ferriter had ceased to be conscious of the priest. His eyes shone wildly and the spots on his cheeks were a brilliant red.

'I didn't discover until the following day,' he continued, 'when she told me herself, in a brazen fashion, that the telephone message she had received while we were having that interview in the sitting-room was from the man with whom she had quarrelled on the previous night. It was after coming back from the telephone in the hall that she kissed me. She was very excited. I suppose she just wanted to share her happiness with me. It is quite easy now to examine things and to find a simple meaning in her actions; but recently it has been quite another thing. Everything has appeared most sinister. When she shed tears during mass, she was probably giving thanks to God for being again united with her lover. And why not? I say now. But at that time I put a different and terrible construction on these things. I happened to look at her when she raised her head after the elevation of the Host. I saw tears streaming down her cheeks. I thought she was saved. Yet I daresay she was just shedding tears of joy at the thought of her lover. Let it be because of that or for some higher motive. I don't care now why she shed tears or why she kissed me. I am no longer angry with her for these things. I realize I should not have interfered. Love is no less noble because its object happens to be base. I was merely guided by my vanity into anger with her when I discovered the truth. You see, father, I want terribly to discover the exact truth, for I have done a terrible thing. Really, I have done a ghastly thing and I want to know why I have done it. Please excuse me, even though this confession is roundabout and confused. You will realize later how important these points are and may God inspire you to give a just judgment.'

'Continue, my son,' said the priest in a respectful tone.

'All that day I tried to get my friends and relatives to help her, but they all turned their backs on me. They were indifferent. The question of saving this drowning person from damnation did not interest them. In the evening I was ashamed to call on her, to tell her the result of my search. I had promised to get her a job. I sneaked past her door and went up to my room, terribly ashamed of having failed her. I was enraged with society and thought our city was another Sodom without any consciousness of God. Until then I had been active in the Catholic movement and I firmly believed that all Catholics were essentially faithful to the principles of Christian philosophy. Now I saw that the Catholic community itself was rotten and must be destroyed with the rest.'

The priest interrupted with some muttered exclamations of reproof, but Ferriter continued in a louder voice, changing back to a whisper when the priest became silent.

'That night I decided as a last resort to marry her. This appeared to me a very desperate thing. Indeed it was partly a gesture of contempt for my relatives. I wanted to humiliate them because they despised me. Very likely there was little in my whole scheme for saving her; this marriage idea as well as everything else was but a cloak for my passions. Yet I want to be just to myself as well as to her, father. Next morning I went to her with the intention of making this marriage proposal. In fact, I took it for granted she would marry me, for I had spent the greater part of the night making plans for the future. Then I received a shock. I learned from her own lips that she had been lying in her lover's arms for the greater part of the previous day and until six o'clock that morning. She was again the brazen harlot. She told me that she had met him immediately after mass. They had patched up their quarrel. She told me not to bother about her. She was quite happy, she said, even if she only had him one night a week. After all I had suffered for her and the proposal I intended making, this news made me want to do something violent. I didn't know what I wanted to do exactly, except, vaguely, to destroy something at once. I came to the conlusion that she was a damned woman and that nothing could save her. She had been drinking and she was still sodden with drink. There was a black rime on her lower lip. She was like a swine. Yet I still felt tender towards her at that time. It was against him that my rage turned first. I reported the whole affair to the vigilance society of which I was then a member. His father was chairman of the committee and because of that no action was taken. They didn't want to have the chairman's son exposed. Then I recognized that the society was another example of our social hypocrisy and corruption. Futile and foul old people using the young enthusiasm of fools like me for their own cunning purposes, so that they might pose as righteous Pharisees.'

'Hush, hush,' said the priest nervously, a little afraid of the angry manner in which Ferriter had begun to speak. 'That isn't the proper frame of mind for a humble penitent craving God's mercy.'

'I beg your padron, father.'

'You spoke of that society and its members in terms of disgust and loathing. Are you still in that state?'

'I'm sorry, father. I was only trying to visualize

my attitude at that time, in order to find out why I came to such a terrible decision.'

'What decision?'

'I decided to kill the woman.'

'My goodness!' said the priest in a tone of horror.

'Yes. I think it was two days afterwards. In the meantime I suffered terribly. Indeed, to be quite true, I had reached a state in which I was hardly aware of what I was doing. You know, one suffers up to a certain point and then a sort of lassitude follows. I remember that I got into a similar state after my father's death two years ago. It seemed that all hope had disappeared and that there was no further incentive to live. Then, on the third night after I had complained, as I was going upstairs, I met her again. She was coming out of the bathroom, dressed just as she was when I . . . just as she was dressed when I . . . the last time I saw her.'

Suddenly he covered his face with his hands and moaned:

'O God! Teresa, why did I do it? I am terribly ashamed.'

'Courage, my son,' said the priest gently. 'Open your heart to God. Let Jesus share your trouble.'

After a little while the murderer regained control of himself.

'That night she looked radiantly beautiful,' he continued, 'but there was a gleam in her eyes which told me that she was mocking me. I must confess that I had said horrible things to her at our last meeting. Now she wanted to injure me for what I had said to her. Perhaps also she hated me for having tried to help her, for she was still ashamed of her life and unhappy. She stood on the stairs in my way, smiling at me in a lewd fashion and saying unclean things. I can't remember exactly what she said, because I was confused by my love for her. However, I was amazed to hear her use a coarse word, which I could hardly believe she was capable of using. I gathered that she was inviting me to her room, not sincerely or out of affection for me, but through bitterness and hatred. She wanted to destroy me. Afterwards I reasoned it out in that way, for I learned a great deal in that time of contemplation. Then I thrust her out of my way and dashed up the stairs. I heard her laugh. After going up two flights I halted and looked back over the banisters at the place where she had stood. She had gone to her room. Then I drew back and leaned against the wall. While I was in that position, a man began to curse nearby, in a room off that landing. He used the same coarse word that she had used. Then I got dizzy, and the idea struck me with great force. I saw that she was evil and that she must be destroyed. I felt stupefied. I went to my room. I didn't think of it any more for a long time, but it was there in my mind all the same, although I didn't think of it. In a sense, the desire to kill her lasted only a moment. It was like a loud sound. It struck into my head and then vanished, just as if I had been struck by something that was both sharp and terribly heavy. Next morning I got up feeling very strong even though I had hardly slept at all. I remained like that for several days, suffering no pain except for a slight throbbing at the back of my head and a heaviness in my forehead. Yet something very extraordinary had happened to me. I was no longer myself but somebody else. I am certain that somebody else had taken possession of me. I ask you is this possible, father?'

'How do you mean?'

'Is it, in your opinion, possible nowadays for a human soul to become possessed by a spirit as in biblical times, either by a good or an evil spirit, and if so, is the soul responsible for what the spirit does while in possession?'

The priest mumbled to himself for a little while and then answered:

'It is difficult for me to answer that question on the spur of the moment. The soul, however, is always subject to possession by Divine grace and also it's in danger of giving way before the temptations of the devil.'

The priest spoke in a lame fashion. He was obviously out of his depth and confused by the strange recital. The murderer scowled. By the priest's voice he recognized that he had to deal, not with a man of culture and subtlety of thought, but with a common fellow robed in a black soutane and stole. Again he remembered how God had appeared in the vision, as a rough boor just like his representative in the confession box.

'I know that it was a spirit that came unto me,' he continued, 'but I don't know even yet whether it was good or evil. I have come to the conclusion that each human soul is the nest of a multitude of personalities, each of which represents a cycle of experience and that the body is the field of battle on which they struggle for mastery. Some are even projected from one soul into another, by the supernatural forces that govern them. That is what I mean when I say that I have been possessed. It's inconceivable to me that I could have begun to plan this thing without having been actively aware of it, if it were I myself that had determined to do it. I must have been made the tool of some other spirit, either natural or supernatural.'

'My son,' said the priest, 'you are now trying to shift the blame for whatever you have done on to other shoulders.'

'No, father. It's for another and more important reason that I want to learn the exact truth, as to who was exactly responsible. I want to know the EXACT identity of the man who murdered this woman, if it was truly murder.'

'Speak simply. Tell your story plainly, without trying to go into these explanations. You may have been in a trance, but that would not lessen your responsibility. Your mind was shocked by an access of violent passion and the trance produced by this shock was due to your giving way in the first instance. You cannot escape the responsibility for whatever you have done in that way.'

'Very well, father. I take the responsibility. It's too late now.'

'Nothing is ever too late. God is eternal. What decision did you come to in this trance?'

'That she must die. The idea remained vague

for about a week. I felt morbidly happy during that time. I felt that I had something wonderful hidden within me, making me strong. I once felt inspired to write a poem and it moved me in the same way. That was the same sort of aching pleasure. It was wonderful to go about having it concealed within me. The troubles of life made no impression while it lived with me. Then it suddenly went away because I lacked courage to write the poem. I felt ashamed because it dealt with the passion of love. Perhaps the idea to kill the woman would have gone in the same way as the poem were it not for another meeting with the doctor. I came across him by chance one day in the street. He scowled at me but he did not have time to accost me or do any violence, as I escaped from him in the traffic. However, later in the day I met another man who is an enemy of mine, a fellow who works for the paper that employed me also and he told me that the doctor was threatening to half-kill me. These were the exact words. It was because of the complaint that I had made about him to the society of which his father was chairman. This threat made me very much afraid, as I imagined also how people would ridicule me and how this story would be bandied about Dublin, as

material for quips and rimes. Already I had
suffered enough humiliation in that way. So
that night I decided that the doctor also must
die. I convinced myself that he was equally
responsible with the woman and that he must be
destroyed.'

'Responsible for what?'

'Not personally, father. Let me explain. I
must tell everything in its proper order.'

Here the murderer grew very confused and
his words became jumbled together incoherently.

'At first I decided to destroy him personally.
That night was the last time, until the other
personality finally departed this morning at two
o'clock, that I was in full possession of my faculties. I take it that a man can be said to be in full
possession of his faculties when he examines a
question, as it were, with several different minds
instead of with one. I remember that my hatred
of him restored my love for her that night, until
dawn, when I passed entirely into the power of
the other personality. At dawn I decided that
both of them must die. I reasoned this way.
I felt that it was his evil influence that was setting
her against me, that she and I had something in
common, but that he was coming between us,
turning our love into hatred. I could see her

arms stretched out towards me and tears on her cheeks, just as at mass that other day; but he stood in the background, grinning like a devil and hypnotizing her. I heard her ask me to kill him, but whenever I urged myself to kill him I grew terrified as in a nightmare. I saw myself sneaking away from him, while he smiled with a contempt that cut me to the bone. He towered over me and patted the biceps of his right arm. Then he drew her towards him and possessed her before my eyes. And she received him with great joy, laughing while he fondled her.'

'Where was this?' said the priest.

'No, no,' said Ferriter. 'This all passed through my mind but it was more real than reality. It was in the agony of watching these caresses that I conceived the idea of killing her and making him pay the penalty. Even then I did not hate her completely as I hated him. I still loved her as she had been when the photograph was taken. However, towards dawn, after great suffering, the girl in the photograph also disappeared, and I passed entirely into the power of the spirit.'

'You mean that you gave way completely to the devil?' said the priest.

'That is not yet proved,' cried the murderer indignantly. 'I want you to understand that I was indifferent at that time whether I myself should be part of the sacrifice or not, so long as the world should be aware of it and the cry go out in warning to all believers.'

'Wait a moment. I don't understand you at all now. What sacrifice do you mean?'

'I am very sorry, father.'

He was now panting loudly. He wiped his forehead with his handkerchief and then added in a voice that had suddenly become distant and very insolent:

'I know now that I should not have come here at all. I am boring you with my theories. Please excuse me. This, of course, is outside your sphere altogether.'

The priest put his eyes close to the grille and stared at him in astonishment. Ferriter's eyes were also close to the grille. The priest drew back hurriedly, after catching a glimpse of the murderer's eyes in the gloom.

'Are you ill?' he said.

Ferriter did not answer. He stared fixedly through the network of the grille, rubbing his forehead mechanically. The priest made a movement as if to open the door of the box. Ferriter snorted and mumbled something. The priest became motionless.

'What is it?' he gasped.

'Nothing,' whispered Ferriter. 'Only . . . just now it came back again. That same feeling.'

'What's that?'

'It all came back. That feeling that somebody was inside me.'

The priest uttered an exclamation and moved again.

'Don't move,' cried Ferriter excitedly. 'You must know what I have done was purely an experiment on my part, in order to prove to myself and to all humanity whether God exists or not. I also wished to prove, in the second place but of equal importance with the first, whether man has a divine destiny.'

'Yes, yes,' said the priest timidly.

'Very well,' said Ferriter. 'If man has a divine destiny he must crush evil from his path. All that is evil must be destroyed or else the good will perish and everything will pass under the sway of Antichrist. All life will become the prey of senseless chance, a savage struggle without purpose, where lust and all the other evil passions triumph over virtue. Do you hear? Keep your ears open and don't fall asleep.'

'I hear,' said the priest.

'I did it in order to set an example,' cried

236

Ferriter, raising his voice and speaking with great arrogance. 'I drew up a statement to be read in court when they arraigned me, if all else failed. But I was weak and I have lost everything. I threw it away. Now all is lost. My sorrow is not that I have killed her and that he has escaped the noose, but that I was a weak instrument and that nothing has been proved or laid bare. Do you understand?'

'I understand,' whispered the priest.

'You lie,' sneered Ferriter. 'You don't understand. You think I'm mad, and you're afraid of me. I know you, wolf in sheep's clothing. That much at least has been revealed to me. I am free of you, black humbug. You are just scavengers, swarming over the country like blackbeetles, mumbling and whispering. I met another of your kind to-day, a miserable hypocrite in whom I once believed. But mark you, the day of your destruction is at hand and men like me, whom you have betrayed, will rise to overwhelm you. Stronger men than I will rise and there'll be no time to prepare the death-trap for the noose. You'll swing on every common thing. Sit still and listen to me. What humiliation! I had dreamt of having the world for an audience and I have only you in a wooden box.'

There was a long silence. The murderer was now watching the priest, lest the man might try to escape from the box. He had completely forgotten about his confession, and he had no idea why he was kneeling in that place. The tension was very great. Then he drew back his head, just as he had done in the bathroom when he was waiting to commit murder. At that time he had been trembling, and the movement had made his body taut. Now it enabled him to relax.

'It's gone,' he said in a tone of surprise.

The priest sighed with relief.

'It's gone,' Ferriter repeated, as if talking to himself. 'Now it's all vague again. I only know that I have killed her. I plunged a dagger in her back and she fell dead across the foot of the bed. She trembled for a little while and then she lay still. She'll never move again. They put her in a coffin and I heard them hammering. I tugged at the knife until it came out, all gory with her blood. What have you to say to me? Why don't you speak to me?'

'You have murdered this woman wilfully?'

'Wilfully? What do you mean? I told you I loved her. How then could I kill her of my own free will. I still love her. Now she is the only one that is dear to me, even dearer than she was before. She is nearer to me and she is purified. Only it's very strange and horrible to feel hunted and outcast like a wild beast. I wished her no wrong. I only wanted to save her. He grabbed her from my hands. Even when I was angry with her it was only through love for her. A father can be angry with a son that is dearer to him than the apple of his eye. Why is it all so incomprehensible? When there is no danger you are all ready with advice, but now you look at me strangely and ask questions. I came here to question, not to be questioned. Can't you have pity on me and be human, whoever you are?'

'Calm yourself, my son,' whispered the priest. 'There is no sin that God will not forgive, if he is approached with contrition and humility. I only asked you if you had murdered her wilfully, because the sin of wilful murder is beyond my power to absolve except in case of extremity or during a Jubilee. Otherwise it can only be absolved by a bishop.'

Ferriter dropped his head and fell into a doze, while the priest continued to explain the rules governing remission of the sin of wilful murder. He had lost interest in what the priest was saying. He felt very tired.

It's all futile, he thought. It matters nothing to me now, whether this man or a bishop hears me. At that moment I lost something precious. They cannot give it back to me. I'm alone with her. They cannot separate me from her corpse as it lay there, with the knife sticking from it. If they could drive away the thought of that knife I could believe in them. But they cannot.

He rose from his knees.

'Where are you going?' said the priest.

'Eh?' said Ferriter.

He knelt down again.

'You can't go like that,' said the priest in an embarrassed tone.

'I came to you in order to find out something,' muttered Ferriter, 'but now the darkness is deeper than ever. You can't raise the dead. It's all a fable, this business of the resurrection. The dead cannot rise again. She MUST lie as I have seen her lie, struck down by my hand. That is the terrible reality. That other terrible reality must also remain. I planned to strike her down, goaded by the torture of my love for her and the constant thought that she lay in his arms. I cannot escape from the knowledge that I planned her death for weeks. Don't keep stirring in your box. You are disturbing me.

Sit still. Yes. I brooded over it. I found great pleasure in rehearsing the act, to the very sensation that I felt when I plunged the knife. I did not, however, rehearse the feeling of complete emptiness which· followed the plunging of the knife. If I had rehearsed that I would never have plunged the knife. Otherwise it was all the same as I had practised in my room, in the bathroom, and in the streets. Often when I was walking I raised my arm and plunged it downward suddenly. I cannot escape from that. It's the truth. Furthermore, no other personality possessed me just now. It was simply my hatred of you all. I hate you like a cringing dog that has been whipped. Even when he wags his tail and crawls on his stomach he feels hatred and merely fawns in fear. Could she rise again from the dead I could humble myself before her and beg forgiveness, but not from you, who are merely some sort of a magistrate. Yes, and only a district one at that. You want to send me to the high court, as if thousands of pounds were involved in this business, and you can only settle cases where shillings and pence are at stake.'

He clutched at the tiny bars of the grille. The priest drew away into the farthest corner of the box and made the sign of the cross between himself and the murderer. Ferriter said in a loud voice:

'I'm glad I hate you. You drove her into the gutter. You all turned away from her after one of you had ruined her. He is one of you. You are all of the same herd, you parasites. The blood of the poor is on your hands and you devour their flesh, you jackals. While I have breath I'll spit on you.'

He drew back and then spat at the priest through the network of the grille. The priest crouched and uttered a cry of terror. Ferriter laughed and got to his feet. He picked up his hat and coat and went towards the door. He paused as he crossed the central aisle. By force of habit he was about to genuflect in obeisance to the Host in the tabernacle. Instead of doing so, he drew himself erect, stared insolently at the tabernacle and then jammed his hat on to his head. Still glaring at the tabernacle, he pulled on his coat. Then he turned abruptly towards the confession box. The priest had opened the door and was looking out furtively.

'What's that?' shouted Ferriter. 'Don't you dare follow me. Do you hear? I'll kill you like a dog.'

The priest drew back into the box. Ferriter

shrugged his shoulders and left the church. Rain was now falling very heavily. A crippled beggar, sheltering beside a pillar of the porch, held out his mug for alms. Ferriter thrust aside the mug.

'Go somewhere else,' he cried. 'There is nothing here. I came here to beg but I found nothing. Nothing at all. Do you hear? Get away quickly.'

Then he rushed down the steps into the rain.

CHAPTER XIV

Soon he was drenched to the skin. The storm was now at its height. Lightning flashed continually. The crashing of thunder rolled in majestic tumult back and forth over the roofs of the city. Streams of water ran along the gutters, carrying whirling refuse on their muddy floods. Tram cars threw up fountains from the hollows by their rails. The drops of rain were so large that they rebounded from the pavements and cut holes into the streams, like shoals of hungry fish cutting the surface of the sea. And like moving shoals of fish, that scurry to the depths in sudden flight to rise again and nose the air near-by, the rainfall changed direction. The content of its downpour lessened or grew big, now dropping soft in a timid shower, now pounding savagely to earth, as if to overthrow a discovered enemy. The wide vault of the firmament had contracted to a tiny space, as if the walls of the universe had given way before invading enemies, who smashed the air into unnatural disorder, with water born of fire,

The murderer was fearless of the storm. He who was usually so timid of a flimsy shower now strolled with coat unbuttoned, grinning at the fierce havoc. Drunk with despair, like a defeated soldier in retreat, who throws away his weapons and his baggage, he found joy in the relief from all responsibility; for now he had no governor, no voice to countermand his inclination towards the most violent extravagance of mind or body. He had cried out at the gates of Heaven for mercy and no one answered. So he was now flying. He was indifferent, like a ship-wrecked man drifting in an open boat at sea, when his swollen tongue has uttered the last cry for help, and he has thrown himself prone among the flopping, swaying bilge, grinning at his fancies. So did the murderer grin and mutter to himself. He had found a new tongue that put curious construction to his thoughts, like a wicked urchin of the deep already settled in the harbour of his doomed mouth, making merry with the prayers of yesterday and changing them to curses that blasphemed all purity and innocence.

He lurched about the slums that bordered to the north of the street where he had done the murder, dragging his feet, stumbling through pools, pausing at corners, seeking a companion

245

for his misery. At last he found her in a narrow lane, into which he prowled, attracted by a cough that came from an open doorway. She smiled on him when he stood before her. Then he ceased to grin and stared at her gloomily in disappointment. At first he waved his hand in disgust and took a pace away from her; but he changed his mind and entered the doorway. Paying no further attention to her presence, he stood beside her motionless, with his eyes on the ground. She examined him suspiciously from head to foot. His hat had become sodden with rain. The rim had fallen limply about his face, concealing all of it except his shark-like jaws and his wide lips. Then he began to sway and she smiled, thinking that his drunkenness was tavern-bred. Putting the stump of a cigarette between her lips, she sucked and then blew a cloud of smoke towards him through her nostrils.

'Good evening,' she whispered.

Startled by the harsh sound of her voice he raised his head but did not look at her or answer her salutation. He blinked, wrinkled his forehead, and licked his lips several times, as if awaking from a swoon. Then he looked at her.

'Good God!' she muttered, awed by his strange eyes.

She was young, but so conditioned by ill-usage that her face had developed the hardness of advanced middle age. She was plump of countenance, with rosy cheeks and a dimpled chin. Her hips and legs were strong like those of a peasant. Yet her dress and posture bore evidence of a dissolute life. An old overcoat, with only one button and that originally a stranger to the garment, was thrown over her shoulders. Beneath it she wore a blue skirt and a yellow jumper. The skirt was torn at the left side and the rent was fastened with a safety pin. Both the skirt and the jumper were heavily stained. The top of a soiled, white under-garment showed at the opening on her bosom. Her breasts were large and sagging. One of her stockings was stitched all up the front of her leg. Her shoes were dirty and torn at the toes. The thumb and forefinger of her right hand were black with nicotine. A little black hat, like an airman's helmet, covered her neck, her ears, and her forehead almost to the eyes. Her face looked terribly inhuman and malicious, a mirror on which all the meaner passions held parade, saluting as they passed, in ignorant servitude.

She grew restless as he continued to stare at her in silence.

'Why are you looking at me like that?' she said.

His lips moved and he waved his arm in the manner of a man trying to find fitting words for the expression of a complex thought. He did not speak however.

'Eh?' she continued, becoming angry. 'What's the matter with me? Have I got horns or what?'

He shook his head and began to mutter, but he could not speak aloud. He felt afraid of her, particularly because she reminded him of Teresa and drew him once more into the endless circle of repentance for which there was no mercy. These were his mutterings, a parody on his confession to the priest, unutterable phrases that flopped about his mouth and found no exit. She threw away the stump of her cigarette, took a pace forward and looked up and down the lane in a bored fashion. Then he sighed deeply.

'Are you a dummy?' she said, without looking at him.

He tipped her on the arm. She looked at him. He smiled and shook his head. She drew her overcoat about her shoulders and prepared to leave the doorway. Then he found tongue.

'One moment,' he said. 'Don't go yet.'

'Well? Ye found yer tongue at last. Are ye drunk?'

'What did you say?'

'Oh! It's deaf ye are. I see.'

'No. I'm not deaf. What did you ask me just now? I'm afraid I wasn't listening properly. Excuse me.'

'I asked ye were ye drunk?'

'I'm not aware of it.'

'Then what's the matter with ye?'

'It would be difficult for me to explain just now. However, for the moment, I beg of you to forgive me, if I have in any way offended you. I want to make restitution for many things and that is one of them. I have often offended people through sheer vanity. In fact, I made a virtue of it. You reminded me of someone, so that I was perhaps too frank, but that can all be arranged later to everybody's satisfaction. At the moment, the important thing is that we should get on terms of friendship and understanding. I want to tell you a number of things that will interest you.'

She was startled more by his conversation than she had been by his silence.

'What are ye doing here?' she said suspiciously.

'I couldn't really tell you off hand,' he said eagerly. 'First of all, we must get acquainted and we must become friends. Then, everything else can come later. Let us say that I'm just wandering about looking for something. It's more correct to say that I'm looking for a thing than for a person. I haven't had time to give it a name yet. You understand, everything must now begin afresh!'

He smiled and rubbed his hands together.

'I'm very pleased,' he said. 'It's just like a man that gets an idea into his head to give new titles to all the books in his library, or rather, to give new meanings to the words in a dictionary. You remind me of her very much, but in a friendly way. What time is it?'

'Aw!' she said in disgust. 'You're too far gone for me. Go home and go to bed, sonny. I bet ye have everything spent except yer tram fare. What time is it?' She yawned, raised her shoulders and added: 'It's nine o'clock. I can see I'll do no good this evening.'

She cursed the rain.

'Nine,' said Ferriter gloomily. 'Then there are still a few hours left.'

'Faith, there isn't a few hours left,' she said. 'Ye're not in London now. They close early here.'

'How do you mean?'

'Aw! Cut it out. Ye're not as drunk as all that.'

'Of course, I'm not drunk, but I don't understand you. Why do you insist on being so violent? I have never injured you.'

She cried loudly close to his ear:

'I'm saying the pubs 'll be closing shortly, so ye better hurry up if ye want to get a drink. Now d'ye understand?'

'Don't speak so harshly to me. I want to be friends with you.'

'Do ye? Well! That's nice. Give us a fag.'

He stared at her and then started, remembering with great pain how he had borrowed a cigarette from Fitzgerald, with the foolish idea of proving some sort of an alibi.

'How stupid the whole thing was planned!' he muttered to himself. 'See how I forgot about the gloves especially. Then it was ordained that I should be caught. Or am I really caught? If I lie and continue to lie, they can do nothing. If I become thoroughly saturated with sin during these few hours, then I can lie perfectly and they cannot put me in the noose. Eh?'

'Haven't ye got a cigarette?' she said. 'Don't ye smoke?'

'It's well known that I rarely smoke,' he said.

'Oh! Is it? I think I have yer mark, me lad. I suppose ye spent yer week's wages on a small port and a biscuit. Good night, Sir Oscar.'

He caught her by the arm and said:

'Wait a moment. I want to go with you. Where are you going? I want to do whatever you like. You know what I mean. Please believe me. If you have seen me before around this quarter and I have in any way offended you, do please forget it. I apologize if I have ever offended you in any way. Let us be friends. Hush! Stand in front of me. I don't want that fellow to see me.'

He hid behind her, as the tiny fellow passed down the lane on the far side. The tiny man was wearing a heavy raincoat, buttoned to his chin and almost reaching the ground. It seemed that he nodded and smiled as he passed the doorway, but his glance was so quick and his expression was so vague that it was difficult to be certain whether he smiled and nodded to Ferriter or was just smiling and nodding his head without purpose. His passage, however, had an extraordinary effect on the murderer.

'What's the matter with ye now?' said the woman.

He was trembling from head to foot, and his face had gone deadly white.

'Look out and see if he is gone,' he whispered.

She looked out into the lane.

'Yes. He's just going around the corner. He's gone now. Why?'

'Nothing. You see, I shouldn't be here, and he knows my friends. He follows me about and he is sure to tell everything I do and everywhere I go.'

'Is that so? God! I'm beginning to think ye're a queer sort of a bloke. Are ye married or what? Maybe ye escaped out of a lunatic asylum. I wouldn't be a bit surprised.'

'It's all right now that he's gone. He didn't recognize me.'

'Ye don't happen to see any snakes on my coat?'

'Eh?'

'Oh! So long. You're nuts.'

'You're not really going,' he said in horror. 'Even you are leaving me. Impossible. You must take me with you.'

'Have you got any money?'

'Of course I have money.'

'How much will ye give me?'

'All I have. I don't want it now.'

'Let's have a look. I hope ye're not kidding me.'

He showed her the silver he had in his pocket.

'Is that all ye have?'

'I have a few pounds in my wallet.'

'Fine. All right. Let's go and have a drink first.'

'One moment. First of all we must get on friendly terms. Tell me your name before we go.'

'Ye can call me Kitty.'

'My name is Francis. Please allow me.'

He took her hand, went on one knee hurriedly, and then raised her hand to his lips. She drew away her hand brusquely.

'For God's sake, pull yerself together,' she said. 'We can't do anything here. Ye should be ashamed of yerself, a young fellah like you, with no control over yerself. Are ye a Catholic or a Protestant?'

'Please don't misunderstand me,' he said. 'You remind me of her.'

'Come on,' she said hurriedly, dragging him into the lane. 'Hang on to me. Then you won't fall.'

'Where are we going?'

'Down to Kane's. It's only around the corner. Tell ye the honest truth, Frank, my tongue was hanging out for a drink when ye turned up. We'll have a couple of quick ones in Kane's and then we'll go somewhere else to have a good time.'

Arm in arm, they lurched through the lane, along a narrow, broken pavement. Then they turned into a wider street that was excessively dirty and almost completely flooded, so that refuse cans had become unmoored and were carried along the channels, their contents spilt and floating on the filthy tide.

'This is Kane's,' she said, trying to drag him through the door of a public-house that stood at the corner of the lane.

But he suddenly resisted her.

'In there?' he asked in horror.

The bar was full to the door. A thick cloud of human breath and tobacco smoke made the light within so dim that the people were hardly discernible. Only a face, or a woman's naked arm protruding gaunt and dirty from a shawl, stood out here and there, as if unsustained in gloomy space and ghoulishly dismembered. The horror of the faces, on each of which disease and debauchery had put monstrous constructions, harried into activity his old fear of sin, so that he drew back like a beast at the door of a slaughter-house.

'What's the matter?' she said.

'I don't want to go in there among those people.'

'We won't stop in the bar. There's a snug at the back.'

'Is there nowhere else to go? This is too dirty.'

During this discussion a group of penniless rowdies, who had been hanging around the door hoping for a chance drink, had drawn near, trying to attract the murderer's attention. They laughed loudly at this last remark. The young woman cursed at them. Then she took Ferriter roughly by the arm and dragged him across the floor. The rowdies pressed about him, begging, claiming acquaintance, warning him against his companion, offering to sell their bodies. They jostled him, staggered against him, trod on his feet, and cursed in his face when he paid no heed. He grew limp — such was his terror; for the nearness of these strange, whispering outcasts bred in his deranged mind the hallucination that he had descended into hell and that these were devils quarrelling over possession of his body.

Then he passed into an inner room. This was a small wooden enclosure at the rear of the bar. It was empty except for the barman, who stood behind the strip of counter, which he was cleaning with a wet rag. The woman placed the murderer on a wooden bench, where he immediately dropped his head between his shoulders and closed his eyes. The barman eyed him suspiciously.

'What's the matter with your friend?' he said to Kitty.

'He got wet,' she said. 'Give him a drop of rum. It'll pull him together.'

The barman shook his head.

'Can't serve him,' he said. 'He's had enough already.'

Ferriter raised his head, looked at the barman and said angrily:

'I think you're referring to me.'

The barman nodded.

'So you think I'm drunk?'

'That's right.'

'Would it surprise you to know that I've never tasted drink in my life and that this is my first visit to a public-house?'

'Tell that to the marines.'

The insolence of the barman roused Ferriter. He got to his feet and strode over to the counter with such arrogance that there could be no doubt of his sobriety.

'How dare you insult me in my present condition?' he cried.

'I don't want to have anything to do with

you,' said the barman a little timidly. 'If the guards came in here and found ye in a helpless condition, it's me that'd get the blame.'

Seeing that the man had become humble, Ferriter changed to a gentle tone.

'Please don't be angry with me,' he said. 'I'm not feeling well, that's all. Somebody very dear to me died this morning.'

'You should have told me that at first,' said the barman.

'Sit down, Frank,' said the woman. 'I'll get ye some rum. Mine is a cherry brandy, Mick.'

While she was bringing the drinks, Ferriter again became confused in his mind. Although his eyes followed the woman, and he understood her presence in so far as her body excited in him a strong desire to blaspheme against God by possessing her, many other conflicting thoughts robbed this desire of all power. It seemed that he was no longer one person, but that he had multiplied into many projections of himself and each projection represented a mood of his personality, arrested in the progress of a particular act or experience, so that he vividly saw himself, in many forms, engaged in all the various phases of the murder, from its conception to the finding of the gloves, and the body of Lavan erect before him, about to utter the formula of arrest; all simultaneous and certain to continue in that state for all eternity.

She came and put a glass of rum into his hand, but he paid no attention to it and still watched her, smiling eagerly in order to conceal from her these threatening projections that were at the same moment plunging daggers, writing manuscripts, listening at doors, hiding behind curtains, tearing up photographs, plotting, hiding under bed-clothes in an attempt to escape from thoughts of Teresa. She poured a little methylated spirits from a small bottle into her glass of cherry brandy. Then she toasted him and put her glass to her lips. He imitated her movements, but made a wry face when the rum touched his lips. The violent stimulant cleared his mind by the unpleasant reaction it caused.

'What's this?' he cried, holding out his glass.

'It's rum. Drink it. 'Twill do ye good.'

'Rum. I'm not allowed to drink alcohol. I have a total abstinence pledge.'

The harlot laughed nervously. Her laughter angered him. He stiffened, put his glass to his lips and tried to swallow all the rum, but he succeeded in drinking only a little of it. It burned his palate.

'Honest to God!' she said. 'I believe ye never drank in yer life.'

'It seems I must make a beginning,' he said fiercely. 'In fact, it is vitally necessary for me,' he added in a whisper.

He continued to sip hurriedly until the glass was empty. Then he sighed and muttered:

'Now God is dead.'

'Who did ye say is dead?'

'When?'

'Ye said someone is dead.'

'Did I? It was a woman I loved.'

'Yer missus, was she?'

'She was no relation.'

'Were ye livin' with her?'

'Only in the same house. She was like you.'

'Was she on the job, then?'

'I don't understand you.'

'Don't ye know what I am?'

'No. Only you remind me of her somehow.'

'Were ye never around here before?'

'I was never in a public-house before.'

'Why did ye want to come with me?'

'Because you reminded me of her.'

'God Almighty! You're very queer. D'ye know what a whore is?'

'Yes. She was a whore.'

'Well! So am I.'

'That's what I mean. I knew you were. I bear you no ill will on that account. That's why I want to go with you, to show her that I bear nobody like her any ill-will.'

'But she's dead,' said the harlot, drawing back nervously.

'I was angry with her for being a whore,' he continued, 'but now I see that I was wrong. In no other way can I make restitution to her than by depriving myself of the advantage I held over her, by throwing away my innocence. The important thing is to love and pity those who suffer. One can do that only by making oneself humble and like the sufferers. I didn't know suffering. I had never suffered until now. Self torture is not suffering. I tortured myself through vanity, because I wanted to be like God. I now see that that is the greatest sin, to torture oneself by unnatural denial, in order to be like God. It must be false. Love is the most noble of all instincts. It's the most gentle too. Only I was afraid of it. I hated it because nobody loved me; so I wanted to prove that it was ignoble and beastly. The god of self-torturers is cruelty and vanity. Such is the god of those who oppress others with their dogmas. I have helped to oppress lovers. I oppressed her terribly. Now I suffer for it. I wanted to make her like myself, because I pretended to know God; but when I searched I found nothing.'

He smiled at her pathetically and added:

'I found nothing at all.'

'Lord!' said the harlot. 'Ye're a terribly eddicated man. Are ye a gentleman?'

He smiled again and said cheerfully, heated by the rum:

'Don't set me apart from you.' He took her hand.' 'I am like you. You have killed something also, something that you were taught to believe should not be killed. I don't know why you did it. Perhaps you did it through some meanness, or through passion, or through a desire for joy and dancing. I always loved things that danced and sang, although I was afraid to take delight in human beings that danced and sang. But I loved the lesser things that were gay, birds and flowers and running water. If they can do no evil by their singing and their dancing and their beauty, neither can human beings, who are really much more beautiful, because they can learn to understand why they are singing and dancing. But here there is no joy. So we both suffer, you and I. We have killed something, each of us, so we are sad and lonely and afraid. Don't you understand?'

He began to press her hand and to wave it to and fro in his, like two peasants singing and trying to form a union of their souls with a hand clasp.

'Janey!' she said. 'Don't talk like that. You put the wind up me. Cheer up, man. There are lots more girls in the world. Have another drop of rum.'

He dropped her hand and suddenly became gloomy.

'Why did she remind me of her?' he muttered, dropping his head between his shoulders.

The harlot shook him and fondled him, trying to rouse him; but he had again become a prey to the strange multiplication of his personality. His mind was again a crazy screen on which the actors, all one character, reeled off the simultaneous film of the murder.

'Give me more rum,' he cried suddenly. 'That's what it's for, isn't it, to make one forget. I keep thinking of her. You musn't speak of her again. I want to forget that. Later on I'll tell you about it, when we have done what we are going to do. We must hurry, because that's expected of me. Here. Take some money and bring me another drink.'

As Kitty was going to the counter, two other harlots entered the room. She said they were friends of hers and asked whether they could have a drink. He agreed. One of them, who announced herself as Madge, did a caper around the floor before him, holding up her outer skirt and showing a number of petticoats, all spotlessly clean and trimmed with fine lace. She wore a shawl, half boots with elastic sides and long ear-rings. Her hair was dressed in the Spanish fashion. Having finished her caper, she made a profound curtsy before the murderer and said:

'I make bold to salute your honour.'

The murderer got to his feet and bowed low before the harlot. They all laughed.

'Elizabeth Mary Ellen is my full name,' said the third harlot, holding up her skirt at the sides and showing a naked thigh. 'I've no petticoats and I'm known as plain Lizzie, but there's a bit of good Mullingar beef for ye.'

She slapped her naked thigh. She had hardly any teeth and matter issued from the sockets of her red eyes. She was tall, thin and shabbily dressed.

'More like the thigh bone of a starved mule,' said Madge.

'Don't you believe her, mister,' said Lizzie. 'There's enough there to warm a regiment.'

She sat beside him on the bench.

Kitty, at the counter, grew jealous of her prey, and insulted Lizzie in a coarse manner. Lizzie retorted still more coarsely. Madge sat on the other side of the murderer and began to show him her petticoats one by one. Kitty returned with the drinks, pushed Lizzie violently aside and sat close to the murderer. Still quarelling, they poured methylated spirits into their cherry brandy and toasted him, becoming indecent in their comments and their promises of pleasure. He grew excited by their conversation and swallowed his rum quickly, but its intoxication made him revolt against the contamination of his company. At first he wished to rise and leave them, but the thought of flight brought to his memory the desert he had seen that morning, where blood flowed in an endless stream through a dead valley. Then he turned on them and said:

'Be silent. I didn't come here for that reason. I had something much more noble in my mind.'

'Oh! Did ye?' giggled Lizzie.

'Don't you be impertinent,' said Kitty. 'Let the gentleman have his say.'

Getting very excited, he made a rambling speech to them about the regeneration of humanity, but they kept interrupting him with ribald remarks, thinking that he was a frequent type of drunkard to be met with in that district – an individual who got religious mania when giving way to the pleasures of debauchery. He broke down at length and submitted to their fondling. The alcohol began to take effect on him. When he had drunk another glass of rum, he grew giddy and began to make childish remarks.

'Do people have fun here, really?' he asked. 'Could a fellow like me have fun here? If I'm good and treat you kindly will you let me play with you?'

They laughed hysterically.

'Begob!' said Lizzie. 'I'll tell you girls what he is. He's a parish priest on his holidays.'

'No,' said Madge. 'He's more like a Protestant parson. The priests go to England where they won't be recognized.'

'Are ye good at making fun?' said Kitty.

'I never had any fun,' he said. 'She kissed me once on the cheek. That was all.'

A roar of laughter followed this remark, and he flushed with shame as a vague memory of that kiss and its effect on him floated through his mind among the deadening fumes of alcohol. Yet he had no power to feel angry with them. Kitty saw him flush, and grew afraid that he might be frightened away by their mocking and that she would lose her prey.

'It's not right to be making fun of the gentleman,' she said. 'He's nearly out of his mind, he was telling me, on account of his tart dying.'

The other harlots made expressions of great sorrow with their eyes and lips.

'Ah! The poor creature!' said Madge. 'And how did she die?'

'She died a terrible death,' said the murderer, shuddering.

'Was it in the Lock she died?' said Lizzie.

In spite of herself Kitty again laughed. The murderer covered his face with his hands. Madge hugged him and said:

'Me poor boy, so ye came looking for a hair of the dog that died.'

'Leave him alone,' said Kitty fiercely. 'That's enough now.'

The murderer burst into tears, whereupon the harlots began a violent quarrel that brought the barman from the outer room.

'Get out of the house,' he cried. 'I don't want any rows on here.'

He shook Ferriter roughly. The murderer jumped to his feet and looked around him wildly.

'Get out of here,' said the barman. 'I've been watching ye for the last half hour. Where d'ye think ye are? In a whore house?'

'How do you mean?'

'I won't allow any filthy goings on here.'

'Do you know who I am?' shouted Ferriter arrogantly.

'I have a good idea who ye are,' cried the barman. 'Ye're a disgrace to a Catholic country. Clear out of here.'

'I?'

'Yes. I'm talking to you.'

'O my God! What humiliation!'

The barman seized the murderer by the nape of the neck and rushed him through the outer room into the street, cheered by the drunken crowd. The murderer slipped on the wet pavement and fell. When he struggled to his feet he found to his astonishment that the tiny fellow was standing beside him. The little fellow was smiling amiably. Moved by a sudden impulse, Ferriter stretched out his hand.

'I'm delighted to meet you,' he cried enthusiastically, shaking the little man's hand.

'I'm really very pleased. Walk along with me a little way. I want to tell you something very important.'

'Yes, sir,' said the little man.

'Listen,' said Ferriter, when they had gone a little way. 'I have made some very important discoveries. I promised Mr. Lavan to find out the exact identity of the murderer, and I think I have done so. I'm very pleased. That's correct.'

'Yes, sir,' said the little man. 'That's right. Enjoy yourself.'

'Keep me well in sight,' continued Ferriter confidentially, 'because my enemies are after me.'

'That's right, sir.'

'Why do you pretend not to know me or believe what I'm saying?'

'Ha! Ha! Very good, sir. Have a good time.'

'Please understand,' said Ferriter, raising his voice, 'that you can't terrify me. I'm no longer afraid of you.'

'It's a bad night,' said the little man. 'We'll have more rain.'

He disappeared into the night. Ferriter looked after him, frowning. All day he had divided his responsibility into two parts, clearly separated — that which he bore to the Church and that which he bore to the State. Until now that which he bore to the Church had been by far the more important — the State being merely something which he had to outwit by every available means. He had understood his act to be something unrelated to society, except in so far as the State was an enemy of the Catholic Church — something to be cleansed and kept in order, duly humbled. Now his relation with the Church was cut off, and the State loomed powerfully before him. The noose of the State dangled over his head.

He saw it dangling, as he stared into the darkness, at the point where the little man had vanished.

The rain had now ceased, but the sky was laden with clouds which sagged so low that the rare lamps made hardly any impression on the darkness. In the forbidding sky he saw a rope suspended. It ended in a noose that swayed back and forth. The rope was blood red. Blood dripped from the noose. Two eyes peered from the cloud above the rope. Then two hands clutched the rope, swung the noose and sent it whirling towards his neck. He shuddered. There was a loud noise in his ears and he gasped for breath. Then he put his hands to his neck to take away the noose. The delusion vanished,

It was one of the harlots who had her arms around his neck. They had come behind him while he stared and they were talking to him, trying to bring him somewhere. Joyfully he embraced one of them with violence. Shouting and laughing, they dragged him along the street to an eating-house.

CHAPTER XV

IT was very warm in the eating-house and the heat made the murderer quite drunk, much to the amusement of the harlots, who now treated him as a harmless buffoon. Indeed he attracted the attention of all the customers by his fantastic behaviour. It was the contrast between his solemn, pathetic countenance and his ludicrous conduct that amused them. His face was deadly pale, and there was an expression of great pain in his sunken eyes, which were still red as the result of his tears in the public-house. He had lost his hat in the street. His fair hair had turned dark with rain. It lay in a sodden glib down over his forehead. His collar had become undone during the horseplay with the women. The end of his necktie hung over his shoulder. They had ordered a meal of fried fish, potatoes and pigs' trotters. He devoured this food with great appetite, using neither knife nor fork. He licked his fingers in a childish fashion, and made foolish remarks in a melancholy voice. The refinement of his voice and speech particularly amused them and they tried to imitate him. He put fish bones in his button-hole. He threw potato chips into the air and then tried to catch them in his mouth as they fell, just like a dog. His hands, face, and clothes became soiled, and one of the harlots, making pretence of putting his dress in order, added to his slovenly appearance by combing his hair with a fish-bone.

When he had finished eating he dropped his head on the table amid the ugly mess he had made. He closed his eyes and began to snore. The harlots roused him, but his head dropped lifelessly as soon as they let go of it. Then they held counsel. Madge suggested giving him methylated spirits. They mixed some in a glass with mineral waters and forced him to drink it. That roused him. He began to splutter and recover a little of his senses. They made him pay the bill and helped him out of the eating-house. He kept muttering unintelligible things; and in the doorway he turned back and tried to make a speech to the other customers about the regeneration of mankind.

In the street, however, he relapsed, and coming to a wall he leaned against it heavily, closed his eyes and seemed to fall asleep. The harlots began to argue among themselves in harsh

s   273

voices. Madge suggested that they should pick his pockets on the spot and leave him asleep against the wall until a policeman found him. Lizzie supported this proposal, but Kitty violently disagreed, maintaining that she had found him, that he was her property, and that she alone had a right to the whole booty. She further maintained that she was an honest woman and that she was anxious to give him amusement for his money. Therefore, she took him around the body and dragged him away with her, telling the other two harpies to go and find a drunkard for themselves. They followed her, however, shouting in her ears that they had often shared their spoils with her when she was in need. The murderer's body being limp, she found it difficult to drag him away quickly, and finally she became so incensed by the gibes of her comrades that she dropped him in the open doorway of an empty house. Seizing Lizzie by the throat she set about her with great force and the two women struggled to and fro, tearing at one another.

Leaving her two comrades to fight it out, Madge tried to escape with the murderer and she had hauled him along a few yards, when she slipped in a puddle and came down heavily, thereby attracting the attention of the fighters. They loosed their hold and both attacked Madge. Suddenly the murderer began to shout, calling for help. Then they united in trying to pacify him, giving him some more methylated spirits, raw from the bottle. They put him sitting against a wall, drew apart and came to an agreement that Kitty was to have him on agreeing to give each of the other two a small share of the profits.

Then they raised him to his feet and brought him around the corner into a drinking shop that had once been a prosperous brothel.

CHAPTER XVI

'HOLY Jerusalem! Look who's blown in. Sacred Francis Ferriter, and he's as drunk as a brewer.'

It was Callahan, the journalist, who had spoken. Standing before the fireplace in the drinking shop, with his hands in his pockets, his hat at the back of his head and a cigarette dangling from his lower lip, he grinned with malicious glee at Ferriter, who had stumbled into the room, accompanied by the three harlots.

Ferriter recognized Callahan. He halted, swayed, and turned on his heel, intending to leave the place, but Kitty held him.

'Stand yer ground,' she said haughtily. 'Sit down near the fire and warm yerself. There's nobody going to interfere with ye while I'm here.'

'So this is what we've come to now,' said Callahan. 'Well! If this isn't more astonishing than the fall of the Bastille I'm a Hottentot.'

'So ye are in any case,' said Kitty. 'And ye're no gentleman either.'

'You shut your trap,' said Callahan. 'I'm not talking to you.'

Ferriter looked furtively at Callahan and then

sank into a chair by the fire. Then he looked helplessly around the room, trying to recover his senses. There were three other men and a woman present, and they were all looking at him. The woman, very old and shabby, sat in a corner behind a table on which she leaned, smoking a cigarette and stirring something in a cup with a fork. The three men were with Callahan. They all appeared to be drunk. Ferriter recognized one of them, a lawyer with whom he had a slight acquaintance. He once had an argument with the man during a riot at a theatre. Ferriter had been one of a group of young Catholics who stopped the performance of a play in which a slighting reference had been made to the Immaculate Conception. The lawyer was a well-known opponent of Puritanism — a fact which prevented his talent from earning him success in his profession.

Meeting Ferriter's eyes, the lawyer nodded gravely.

'We meet again, Mr. Ferriter,' he said.

'And with a vengeance,' said Callahan.

'The vengeance is certainly mine,' said the lawyer.

'Something else 'll be yours unless ye mind yerself,' said Kitty.

'See that?' said Callahan. 'The apostle of righteousness has raised an army of whores to defend him against his godless enemies.'

'Yes, Mr. Ferriter,' said the lawyer. 'The circumstances are very different from our last meeting. I remember you called me a drunken pagan. Now you appear to be drunk yourself, and your three concubines suggest that you have turned pagan.'

'I'll be damned if I can get over it,' said Callahan. 'Tell us the sad story, Frank. How did it happen? When I left you this morning you were still in the odour of sanctity. A stinking odour it was, too. You were a proper, smelly, little skunk. I've a good mind to warm your pants for what you said to me.'

'You'll behave yourself, mister,' said Kitty, threatening Callahan with her fist, 'or I'll give you what you're looking for.'

'Get out of my way, you pox bag,' said Callahan roughly.

The harlot got into a rage. She and her two comrades began to abuse Callahan, but the proprietress entered the room with some drinks and silenced them.

'What's on here?' she said in a gruff voice.

'It's all right, Biddy,' said Callahan. 'These

birds got hold of a craw-thumping Johnny called Ferriter, made him tight and brought him in here. There he is.'

'Who is he?' said the proprietress, putting some glasses on the table.

'Ever see the lad before?' said Callahan. 'He's a vigilance society man. He's probably been around here many a time with Tim O'Leary's fancy men, raiding the kips and making the whores join the Children of Mary.'

'Is he one of that crowd?' said the bawd, curling her lips.

'Indeed, he is,' said Callahan. 'I know him very well. You better be careful of him. He looks tight, but he might be gamming on, so as to be able to give us all away. He might be scouting here.'

'He's a gentleman,' said Kitty. 'Don't pay any attention to him, Mrs. Shea.'

'Yes. He's a gentleman,' said Madge and Lizzie, eager to defend their share of the loot.

'A gentleman, is he?' said the bawd. 'Is that right what ye told me, Mr. Callahan? Is he one of them vigilance men? If I thought he was I'd take him by the seat of his pants and chuck him to hell out of here. God's curse on them. They've ruined me.'

'He's one of those prime boys all right,' said Callahan. 'Heave him out. We don't want his company.'

'Leave him alone,' cried Kitty. 'Mrs. Shea, make that fellah leave my friend alone. We were drinking in Kane's. He only had a couple, but he's not used to it. A friend of his died this morning and he's cut up about her.'

At this Callahan roared out laughing.

'A friend of his died this morning, eh?' he cried. 'A friend of his? Is that the idea? I'll tell you why he took to drink. It's because he tried to do me a dirty trick and he got the sack for his pains.'

'I think he's honestly drunk, Jack,' said the lawyer. 'Leave him alone. Give him a chance to reform. It's never too late to mend.'

'That's right, sir,' said Kitty. 'Tell yer gentleman friend to keep his mouth shut and to behave himself.'

Callahan spat his cigarette into the fire, leaned over Ferriter and said:

'So you wouldn't give me any information about the murder, wouldn't ye? Ye ran to Corish with all your dope and then he sacked ye? Now you are prowling about the kips telling everybody she was a friend of yours. You are a proper bloody swine. I wouldn't bet much on your chance of living if Mick O'Leary gets hold of you.'

'Leave him alone, Jack,' said the lawyer. 'It's better to ignore those fellows. Nothing irritates them so much as contempt. If you abuse him you merely do him a favour. He's earning ten thousand days' indulgence for himself for every word of abuse you utter. They have a marvellous technique of self-torture.'

At this Ferriter raised his head and stared at the lawyer. He did not speak, however.

'Will I tell her to bring four bottles of stout, Frank?' said Kitty. 'It's the only thing ye can get here. They have no rum.'

'Fleecing the Lamb of God?' said Callahan.

'Why do you keep butting in?' she cried.

'Bad and all as he is,' said Callahan, 'he's in the same line of work as myself, so I'm a friend of his if he needs my help. That's my motto. I'm not going to let you fleece him.'

'You're no friend of mine,' said Ferriter angrily.

'That's one in the eye for you, mister,' said Kitty.

'Here. Take this,' said Ferriter, giving her a pound note. 'Get what you want.'

'And don't forget the change,' said the lawyer.

'I'll take no interference from you either,' said Ferriter.

'You wouldn't be looking for a fight by any chance?' said Callahan in a sinister tone.

'Let's have no rows, Jack,' said one of the other men.

'Whatever row is made here, I'll make it,' said the bawd, changing her attitude towards Ferriter on receipt of the pound note. 'Stout for four is it?'

'I don't want to fight,' mumbled Ferriter. 'I don't want any sympathy either. I just want to be left alone with my friends. I came here for a certain purpose. Your persecution won't prevent me doing what I want to do.'

He took Kitty by the hand and looked defiantly at the lawyer.

'Hear, hear!' cried the lawyer, striking the table. 'That's a sound philosophy. What progress even the most backward pupil makes in the school of alcohol! Let's hope that in future, when you are playing the role of whore-hound, you won't forget this night when you are playing the more amusing role of whore-master.'

'Your language is coarse,' muttered Ferriter thickly, but with an attempt at being insolent.

At that the lawyer burst into a fury and cried: 'What audacity! But it's typical of your kind. You damned hypocrite! It's on a par with the stockbroker that turned his dead son's photograph to the wall when he had a lady to bed with him. You sex-starved slave! You can't drink without making a pig of yourself, and then you'll go to confession to-morrow, become purified by the waving of a thumb and forefinger and then . . . Lo and behold! You're all ready to start again burning books, raiding soldiers and their tarts on the canal banks, prying into chemists' shops for contraceptives.'

'I won't allow you to talk like that,' cried Ferriter, becoming a little more sober. 'You don't understand why I'm here. Is this your alternative – this Hell? I want to do away with this too.'

'D'ye hear the son of a gun?' said Callahan. 'He'll start preaching to us in a minute. Drunk, dirty and debauched in the custody of three whores, and yet he has the cheek to preach to us.'

'That's the amazing thing about them,' said the lawyer. 'They suspect that they are losing something wonderful by being afraid to fornicate in brothels. They imagine they are losing some wonderful sensation through their greed of

Heaven. That's why they hate us unbelievers. They really don't believe in Heaven, so they are afraid we may escape punishment in the next world for our libidinous pleasures in this. Pleasures! Does any fool think there is pleasure here? If you have ever been to a bull ring, you'll see old jaded horses driven out blindfold to be torn by the bulls. They are a cruel parody of noble animals. So are the unfortunate women that come here. I'm here because I'm bored. I feel I have to make some gesture of revolt or go insane. I visit this slimy catacomb as a gesture of revolt against the intellectual stagnation forced on me by the damned horde of Puritans of which you are a member. I'd rather be at a good theatre, or in my study with a good book, or in bed with a woman I loved. But you'll allow me none of these. That's why I'm here. It's not I but you and your kind that bring brothels and whores into existence, shebeens and slums and crime and disease. All these things grow out of your miserable greed, your cruelty and your meanness.'

While the lawyer had been speaking, Ferriter had watched him eagerly, moving his lips and nodding assent. Then he said quietly:

'I admit I was wrong. Am I not to be forgiven? I came here to make restitution.'

Callahan laughed.

'What?' he said. 'Did you think you were depriving the poor of their just wages in breaking up the kips?'

'I wasn't speaking to you,' said Ferriter with dignity. 'You are just a shallow nature. The hypocrite and the libertine are but two sides of one picture. I had a vision of beauty,' he con-continued, raising his voice, 'and even though I have failed in my purpose and could not find that beauty down the road I followed, I still believe there is such a thing. I believe that man shall one day reach a state of supreme virtue and beauty. While following the wrong road towards that goal, I injured one of these.' Here he bowed to Kitty. 'As the woman I injured is dead, I have come to make restitution to her, by giving myself to one as unfortunate as herself.'

'You sanctimonious hypocrite,' said Callahan.

Ferriter staggered to his feet.

'Let him speak,' said the lawyer. 'This is interesting. Let's get our money's worth in kind. It would greatly help to brighten these desolate places if the vigilance society sent one of their preachers here every night.'

All the men laughed, and Ferriter became violently excited. Yet he spoke in a restrained tone.

'Why do you insist on believing that I'm still a member of that society? I now want to be friends with all of you.'

'Hear, hear,' said the lawyer in mock gravity. 'Do you refuse me a hearing?'

'On the contrary, I'm encouraging you.'

'Man is divine,' shouted Ferriter. 'There is no higher god than this human divinity.'

'Bravo!' cried the lawyer. 'So the news that God is dead has at last reached the Dublin Vigilance Society. Now we may expect startling developments.'

'Please listen to me,' shouted Ferriter. 'I want to tell you that . . .'

'Aw! Buzz off,' said Callahan. 'You dirty swine, you tried to fasten that murder on a pal of mine.'

'Drink up,' said the proprietress, coming from a spy-hole in an outer room, where she had been examining the approaches to the house. 'There's a couple of detectives outside. That little wart, Tyson the spotter, is with them. Hurry up.'

She gave Ferriter his change. He put it in his pocket and handed her back the glass of stout which she gave him. He was about to speak to Callahan when she interrupted him, forced the glass into his hand and urged him to drink.

He swallowed it with difficulty, making grimaces. Callahan and his friends continued to jeer. Then he dropped heavily into his chair, letting the glass fall to the floor. He closed his eyes.

'Jasus! He's passed out again,' said Madge.

'Not at all,' said the lawyer. 'He's in an ecstasy.'

'Take him out of here,' said the proprietress. 'Get out of here. I don't like your sort.'

'Leave him to me,' said Kitty.

Helped by her friends, she took Ferriter off the chair.

'You have the regular cut of a murderer yourself,' said Callahan viciously, as Ferriter stared at him.

'A murderer,' muttered Ferriter thickly.

Then he shook off the harlots, came over to Callahan and whispered in his ear:

'I injured you also. I'll make restitution. Be there at midnight.'

'Where?' said Callahan in astonishment.

'You'll have the full story,' whispered Ferriter, his words almost unintelligible. 'I'm making restitution to everybody I have injured.'

Then he staggered out of the room with the harlots. There was a roar of laughter when he went, but Callahan did not join in this laughter.

'God Almighty!' he said to the lawyer. 'Who would have thought it?'

'What?'

'It was he himself that did it.'

'That did what?'

'Nothing. Good night, lads. I'm off.'

'What's happened?'

'Double headlines for to-morrow's paper.'

CHAPTER XVII

THE murderer and the three harlots went down the street, followed on the far pavement by the little man and two detectives. Two streets farther on the harlots brought the murderer into a house that was partially in ruins. There was no door to the hallway. It was pitch dark in there. There was a foul smell. One of the women lit a match. They began to climb a broken stairway. Before they had mounted many steps, a door opened on the floor above.

'Who's there?' said a woman's voice.

The harlots answered.

'All right. Come on up.'

They entered a room on the first floor. The door was immediately bolted behind them. It was stiflingly hot in this room, as the windows were closed and there was a large fire in an open grate. There were two beds, one to the left of the door, another in an alcove to the right. Two children slept in the bed on the left. Their little heads lay side by side on one pillow. One child's chubby arm encircled its companion's neck. They slept peacefully, and their breathing was not disturbed by the entrance of the murderer and his companions.

'Don't make any noise,' said the hag who had opened the door. 'The kids are asleep.'

This hag was barefooted. She was very fat, and her grimy white hair had fallen down her back in a tousled plait. She waddled over to a cupboard, her hands clasped on her large stomach.

'Where's Jack?' whispered one of the harlots.

The hag pointed to the bed in the alcove on the right.

'He's come in with a bit of a jag on him,' she muttered.

A man with a bald head lay on his back, fully dressed, in this bed. His mouth and right eye were wide open. Yet he was asleep and snored loudly at every third or fourth breath. His knees were drawn up and his wet boots had made black tracks over the coverlet. His left hand, still holding a tattered cap, was flung out towards the end of the bed.

'Pull up to the fire,' whispered the hag to Ferriter.

He had stood near the door, watching the sleeping children, who seemed to hypnotize him. When the hag spoke he started and then walked on tiptoe to the fireplace, still glancing furtively towards the children. He sat down beside Kitty on a form to the right of the fire. The other two women sat opposite.

'Stout ye'll have, sir?' whispered the hag.

Kitty answered her. Ferriter continued to stare at the children.

'What's the matter with ye?' whispered Kitty in his ear.

'Who are these children?' said Ferriter. 'Why are they here?'

'They live here?'

'They really live here?'

He looked in wonder at the hag.

'She's their grandmother. Their mammy is in clink. She got three months for lifting a roll of cloth. That's their dad in the other bed. Don't be afraid of him. He's a quiet man.'

'But we shouldn't be here in the children's house,' he said nervously.

Madge leaned over and whispered lasciviously: 'Have a look at these.'

She raised her skirt and showed him indecent designs embroidered on an inner petticoat. Lizzie made a bawdy remark.

'Hush!' he said angrily. 'There are children here.'

'God!' said Kitty. 'Maybe that fellah was right after all. Are ye a member of some vigilance society? Are ye spying on us?'

'What's that ye're saying?' whispered the hag from the cupboard, where she was pouring stout from a jar.

'It's a lie,' said Ferriter. 'I'm not a member of a vigilance society and I'm not spying.'

'I hope ye're not,' said the hag.

'Please believe me,' said Ferriter, getting to his feet.

'Sit down,' said Kitty, 'we're only kidding ye.'

He sat down and took her hand.

'But why does everybody go on suspecting me?' he cried. 'I've been driven from one place to another. Nobody wants to be friends with me. I could understand that before, for I now confess to you that I was a member of a vigilance society.'

'Oh! So it's true then?'

They all looked at him excitedly, with anger in their eyes.

'But I'm not a member now,' he said hurriedly. 'I swear to you I have no connection with them. Let me explain.'

''Faith if I thought ye were. . . .' began the hag, coming towards him aggressively.

'I swear to you I'm not,' cried Ferriter. 'I have

renounced them all. In fact I no longer believe in God.'

'Is that so?' said the hag.

'That's true. There is no God.'

'None of that now,' said Kitty. 'Who in the name of God d'ye take us for? We're all good Catholics here. We won't listen to any talk like that. By Jesus! I'll have nothing to do with ye if ye're an atheist. I might be swallowed up.'

Ferriter looked around him in a puzzled manner, astonished by the hostility he aroused by declaring that God did not exist. They all declared their faith in God with Kitty, and swore devotion to the Roman Catholic Church.

'Then you all believe in God?' he said.

'Is it heathens ye took us for, then?' said the hag.

'But it's all wrong, then,' he said.

'What's all wrong?'

'I shouldn't be here.'

'Where did ye think ye were?'

'With the damned.'

He had said this in such a serious tone, which warred so outrageously with his dishevelled appearance, that the statement became ludicrous. The women looked at him for a moment or two in astonishment and then by common consent they burst out laughing. At first the hag tried to restrain them, but soon she herself joined in this extraordinary merriment. The murderer made gestures of protest, but his gestures merely excited them further. Then he covered his face and shuddered.

Since coming into the room he had fallen into a state of grave uneasiness. The alcohol which he had drunk had now gone to his head, producing a state of nervous tension exactly opposite to his recent stupor. Under the influence of this tension, all the objects in the room had become very vivid, the children, the bald man, the barefooted hag, the naked floor covered with dark patches. The whispering had awed him and made him expect the imminence of disaster. Now the laughter of the harlots completely routed his self-control and he abandoned himself to fear; especially when the children woke up and began to wail, disturbed by the laughter, and the bald man began to curse in his sleep, tossing his drunken limbs about the bed.

Like a timid man, alone in a haunted house and waiting, against the efforts of his defeated will, for a sign on the wall, or the swish of an unseen shroud, or the ghastly sound of a footfall, he waited for the unknown menace to come near and grasp him. Now he knew that he would screech for mercy when it came, and he wanted to hide from it. But where?

Suddenly he gripped Kitty by the arm and said:

'Take me away from here. I want to be alone with you.'

They answered him with a chorus of lewd remarks. The drunken man sat up in bed and yelled. The children began to wail for their mother. Ferriter jumped to his feet, put his hands in his hair and cried out in a pitiful voice:

'Have mercy on me! Have mercy on me!'

'Be quiet will ye,' cried the hag, running to the window and pulling back the tattered curtain. 'I knew it. They're outside watching. Take that man away.'

'Yes, take me away,' cried the murderer.

'Who's there?' shouted the drunken man.

'There's detectives watching across the road,' whispered the hag. 'Out with that lad. Here, pay for that round of drinks before ye go.'

'Wait till I get hold of the robber,' growled the drunken man, lurching off the bed and rolling on to the floor with a great clatter.

'Give me the money,' said Kitty.

'Don't forget what ye promised, Kitty,' said Madge.

'Haven't I always acted on the square?' said Kitty.

'Take me away,' whimpered Ferriter.

'Give her the money. Give her the money.'

The children continued to wail for their mother, and the drunken man hurled a chair that crashed into the delph on the dresser. Then Kitty dragged the murderer from the room.

CHAPTER XVIII

SHE fumbled about on the landing. It was pitch dark there. Then he heard the creaking of a door being opened. The door was on one hinge and it opened only a little way. She dragged him after her through this opening into a room. Here also it was pitch dark.

'Is there no light?' he said.

'Hush!' she said. 'What d'ye want with a light?'

'I don't like this darkness. I'm afraid.'

'Hold yer tongue. Don't let anybody hear ye. He'll be after us if he hears ye.'

'Who?'

'Jack that was asleep in the other room. There's a woman sick in the next room, too. We'll lie on this bed. There's a bed here.'

'I can't see.'

'Hold on to me.'

There was a rank smell. She led him across the floor to a bed that rattled when she touched the footrail.

'Here it is. Sit down quietly. It creaks terribly. I'll put the mattress on the floor. Wait a minute.'

'Oh! Can't we have a light? I hate this darkness.'

'Be quiet, can't you?'

She pulled at the mattress, but the bed creaked so much that she desisted.

'Better leave it where it is. Sit down here.'

The bed sagged and creaked under their weight.

'Are we safe here?' he said.

'We're all right,' she said, fumbling with her clothes.

'Can they find us here?'

'Hurry up. We haven't much time.'

'But we must stay here. You must stay with me. You must protect me.'

She stopped fumbling and said:

'Eh? What d'ye mean?'

'I want to tell you all about it.'

'Hold on a moment. Let's have my little present.'

'What do you mean?'

'Money. How much have ye got?'

He took the silver from his pocket. She felt the coins in the darkness.

'That's only six bob. What's in that wallet? Let's have a look.'

She deftly rifled the wallet and took his remaining pound note.

298

'Are ye sure ye haven't some more in yer other pockets?'

She rifled his other pockets.

'That's all,' she said coldly. 'Well! Hurry up, now. We can't stay here.'

She lay down and tried to pull him with her, but he resisted, trembling violently.

'But I want to tell you about it first.'

'Oh! Hurry up.'

'But this is too gross.'

The harlot sat up and said harshly:

'D'ye think I'm going to hang around waiting for ye all night?'

'Please listen to me first.'

'Hurry up then.'

'I want to make restitution to you for having injured Teresa Burke, whom I murdered this morning with a dagger.'

The harlot gasped and then said:

'Jesus, Mary and Joseph.'

'I want you to say you forgive me for having done this and afterwards I'll give you my innocence. I murdered her because she tried to take my innocence. I am now sorry I killed her and I beg you to forgive me. Do you forgive me?'

'What have I here?' gasped the harlot. 'A bloody murderer?'

'Forgive me. Oh! Please forgive me. I am heartily sorry for my sin.'

He clutched at her dress and kissed it.

'Keep away,' she gasped. 'God's curse on you, you bloody murderer.'

She struck at him in the darkness and then jumped off the bed. Again he muttered:

'Forgive me. Oh, please, please forgive me.'

He heard her struggle through the opening of the door and then he got to his feet.

'Give me a light,' he muttered, stretching out his hands. 'I want light. I'm afraid. Protect me from this darkness. Teresa, where are you?'

Now there was absolutely no sound, yet he became aware that there was somebody with him in the room. Yet he did not feel afraid. He was staring towards the wall opposite the bed, and he knew that the person was behind him, standing at the foot of the bed, tucking the clothes under the mattress. Then he started and said:

'It's you, Teresa, isn't it?'

She continued to arrange the clothes, taking no notice of his question.

'What do you want me to do?' he said after a pause. 'It's too late now, it seems.'

Still she continued to arrange the clothes, paying no heed to him.

'Why do you ignore me? Won't you speak? Do you refuse to recognize me?'

She paid no heed. Then he cried out:

'I'll make you speak to me.'

He whirled round, raised his right hand above his head and struck at her bended back. His hand struck the iron footrail of the bed. The bed creaked violently. He began to shout, threatening the darkness with his clenched fist. His words were incoherent. His voice was broken and strident like that of a barging woman.

Then heavy steps came up the stairs. The door was thrown open with a crash. A torch was flashed in his face. The murderer's words became coherent and he cried out:

'Don't take me to see him. Please leave me here. I don't want to suffer any more. I didn't mean to hurt anybody. I'm too young to die.'

They had to sit on his back and pour cold water on his head until he grew calm. They handcuffed him and led him from the house. A crowd had gathered outside. They jeered and cursed at him as he was taken away.

CHAPTER XIX

LAVAN was waiting at the police station. He was in evening dress, having just come from a dance. He showed no sign of surprise at Ferriter's disreputable condition.

'Why these handcuffs?' he said to the detective.

'He got violent, sir.'

'Take them off.'

'Thank you, Mr. Lavan,' said Ferriter.

He was very calm. He held himself in a dignified manner, erect and at his ease. He did not look at all afraid of Lavan or of the detectives, or of the sombre atmosphere of the police station. Even when he was formally charged with the murder, warned and asked had he anything to say, he still remained calm.

'I have nothing to say,' he answered in a low voice.

Lavan sat down facing him and began to tap his knees with the tips of his fingers.

'That so?' he said. 'You have evidently forgotten what you promised me.'

'What did I promise you?'

'That you would deliver the murderer into my hands at midnight.'

'I don't remember making any such promise.'

'Oh, yes, you did. You said you wanted to remain free for a few hours in order to find out the exact identity of the murderer. Have you done so?'

'I have nothing to say,' said Ferriter. 'You can do nothing further to me.'

'So? You have no explanation to offer for the blood on your gloves. I may tell you that we have had them examined since and compared the blood with that on the dagger. It was the same blood.'

'That's a lie. I don't believe you. You have no evidence against me. You planted those gloves in my room. You are hired to persecute me.'

'So? I may tell you that we found something further in your room after you left. A manuscript that was lying on the floor.'

At this Ferriter opened his eyes wider. His forehead twitched, but after a few moments he smiled and his face became impassive. He said nothing.

'I think you're very foolish to take up this attitude,' said Lavan in a very friendly tone.

'There are probably extenuating circumstances that would go a very long way towards influencing the court and the public in your favour if you made a clean breast of everything now and got us on your side. The police can do a lot. We want to help you, but if you insult us and continue to regard us as your enemies, our hands are tied. In fact, if you refuse to take us into your confidence, we are forced to assume a hostile attitude. I have nothing against you, my dear man. As a matter of fact, I like your type: a young fellow with a fine sense of his social duties. Yours is the type we want in order to build up the country. If I may say so, although it's going beyond my usual custom to express any opinion on such a controversial matter, we need a healthy and constructive sort of Puritanism in our present stage of social development. A young community like ours needs stern discipline in its morals and in its social character. You'll agree with me there, I hope? There are many abuses that we need to root out of our social system. Young men like you are the very stuff to do it. I may tell you that it was on that account that I was loath to take any action when you raided the bookshop on the quays and burned that poor man's property.'

Here his voice assumed a tone of fatherly reproach. In spite of his determination to resist the wiles of the superintendent, Ferriter began to become affected.

'I am sorry now I didn't warn you at that time,' continued Lavan in a tragic voice. 'I might have been able to open your eyes in time to the dangers of the course you were pursuing. Look at it like this.'

He drew a little nearer and tapped his left palm with his right forefinger. Ferriter could now smell the perfumed oil in Lavan's glossy hair. That and the general spruceness of the superintendent further affected him favourably, It seemed good to him to be in the company of this neat and respectable police officer, who talked so brilliantly and in such a moral and friendly manner, after the squalor, the drunkenness, the foul language, the vice of the quarter which he had just quitted.

'Look at it like this,' continued Lavan. 'We have had in this country for too long a tradition of antagonism to the State and to the servants of the State. That was only to be expected from a people governed for centuries by a foreign ruling caste. We have also come to regard the State as the enemy of the Church. All this has had many evil results. We have come to regard poverty and suffering as the normal condition of all God-fearing men. It developed in us a suspicion of prosperity and amusement. That is correct. A sensitive fellow like you – forgive me for having to be personal – wants to set everything right at once, and being rather unfortunate in your life, the general tendency of Puritanism became exaggerated in you. I had to make enquiries. Please don't think that I'm taking liberties with your private history just to amuse myself or to illustrate a point in my argument. Through your irritation with your misfortunes, you were thrown into the arms of these Puritanical organizations, which were governed by entirely different types. You found them, when it was too late, to be mean and ambitious hypocrites. That is so. You found that they tried to usurp the duties of the police in putting down vice, simply in order to bring credit to themselves, so that they could pose as Christians of the most virtuous type. That was proved to you, was it not, when you reported Dr. O'Leary to your committee?'

Ferriter nodded a trifle eagerly. Lavan came still nearer. He now assumed the manner of an excited political agitator, who is whispering his propaganda into the ears of a prospective convert.

'Naturally,' he continued, 'as a sensitive and honest man, that made your blood boil. Could I blame you? My God! Even though I'm a public servant and I must act impartially towards all parties in questions of this sort, they make my blood boil too. If it weren't for my position, I'd speak my mind to you freely and I'd tell you that, in my opinion, this particular incident is the most damnable indictment of these people. This man, posing as a Puritan and yet shielding his own son. He refuses to set the machinery of his organization in motion, because it was his own son who was concerned in these immoral transactions. It's no wonder you were driven to despair. I can quite understand it. Upon my word I sympathize with you. But the unfortunate part of the story is that you didn't seek the aid of the police at that point. That's where this cursed mistrust of State authority that is ingrained in our people got you into trouble. As I have told you already to-day, I have a very proper respect for my religion. So has every decent man. When I find anybody becoming violent against the Church, or the clergy, or religion in general, I become suspicious of that man. It's bad taste in the first place.

In the second place, it's a symptom of an anti-social disease. But there is a vast difference between having a proper respect for religion and allowing the clergy to usurp the civil power. That is wrong, and I'll have none of it. I'm a servant of the State, and it's my duty to see that the laws of this State are enforced. That's why I have to arrest you and charge you with this murder and see that you are punished with the utmost penalty that the law demands for such an offence, if you persist in your present attitude. Please understand what the utmost penalty is for a crime of this kind. You must surely be aware that the penalty is death. Death by hanging, a most horrible and awe-inspiring death.'

Lavan was now very close to Ferriter. The murderer was looking at the ground, but he could feel Lavan's eyes probing his face, drawing him forward, breaking down the defences of his will. He exerted all his power to maintain silence, but the effort was becoming increasingly painful; especially as the desire for confession and forgiveness had been excited afresh by the friendliness of Lavan's tone, so different from that of the priest, the men in the drinking shop, and the harlot in the dark room. His mind wished to surrender and confess and be forgiven.

308

But his instincts warned him to resist and keep silent.

'Come now,' said Lavan, suddenly drawing back and crossing his legs. 'Now that you understand my point of view, let's discuss the matter as friends, or at least as fellow citizens. Forget that I'm here as a police officer. I think I've given you a sufficient guarantee that I'm something different from a callous machine without humanity.'

He took out his cigarette case and leisurely lit a cigarette.

'So?' he continued. 'I'm damned sorry you did this, Ferriter. Very sorry indeed. Furthermore, you're making it very difficult for me to help you, by not telling me the whole facts of the case. For instance, the extraordinary document that I found in your room might be a great help to you, if you explained to me how that queer idea got into your head. Who influenced you in the first place into coming to the conclusion that wrong-doers should be eliminated by indiscriminate lynching? You don't look a monster, and I feel sure that you are naturally a kind man who wouldn't deliberately hurt any living thing. This monstrous idea must have been inspired by others. Don't you see? They've been using you.

They made you their tool. That's correct. Don't you agree with me?'

Then Ferriter raised his head and spoke.

'Yes,' he said in a strange tone, as if repeating something by command. 'They made me their tool.'

'Of course they did,' said Lavan energetically and with a show of anger. 'They made you their tool and then they slunk into hiding, leaving you to do their dirty work. I bet you weren't aware that they were pumping their pernicious propaganda into you. You don't, by chance, remember any occasion when you heard that suggestion made? Or perhaps you read it somewhere?'

'Yes,' said Ferriter. 'I remember now that I heard this suggestion made several times. I also read something on the subject in a magazine.'

'The *Vanguard*, I suppose?'

'No. It was another paper that ceased publication by order of the archbishop.'

'Was it *The Templar?*'

'Yes. It was the official organ of the Knights of the Temple.'

'A kind of secret military society that a man called Traynor started a few years ago?'

'Yes. It was started during the religious persecution in Mexico.'

'You were a member of that organization?'

'I didn't actually join it, but I had many conversations with a schoolmaster called Brabazon on the subject. He believed very strongly in this doctrine. At that time, however, the idea of shedding blood revolted me.'

'Very naturally,' said Lavan. 'Did he make any particular suggestion?'

'Yes. He proposed that we should kill a certain writer who had just written an obscene and blasphemous book.'

'And you very properly refused?'

'Yes. I thought he was going too far. The idea revolted me at that time.'

'I suppose you know that Brabazon is now in a lunatic asylum, after having tried to murder his sister-in-law?'

'I had not heard of it.'

'I can tell you something about Traynor too. He was purely an unscrupulous adventurer. I have reason to believe that he has since become an agent of the Soviet Government, operating in Great Britain.'

'That may be so. I repeat that his ideas

revolted me at that time. I had nothing to do with him.'

'Still, his ideas must have influenced you, because what you have written goes to prove that the idea of religious assassination must have lain in your mind for a long time. Even if the idea revolted you, you felt strongly on certain questions. That is correct. You will agree with me?'

'Yes. I admit that I sympathized with certain sacrifices made by Catholics in Mexico.'

'What do you mean by sacrifices?'

'The killing of government officials and other notorious persecutors.'

'I wouldn't use the word sacrifice to denote assassination if I were you,' said Lavan. 'It would prejudice the court against you.'

'What court?' said Ferriter in alarm, suddenly realizing that the conversation was drifting into dangerous channels.

'In this country,' said Lavan, flicking the ash from his cigarette, 'assassination, whether religious or political, has come to be looked upon with the horror it deserves, as the final abomination. You had better use the word *murder*. It's at least more human.'

'I don't understand you,' said Ferriter.

His eyes were dilated. His chest heaved.

'For goodness sake,' said Lavan, 'keep your wits about you and help me to draw up your defence. I'm trying to find out exactly who has instigated you in the first place to commit this murder.'

'What murder? Did I say I committed a murder?'

Lavan threw out his arms in a gesture of despair.

'It's hopeless trying to do anything for you,' he cried. 'You admit a thing at one moment and you deny it at the next. At one moment you discuss calmly and clearly how the idea to commit this murder got into your head and then at the next moment you ask me. . . .'

He was interrupted by a gesture from the murderer, who at that moment surrendered, unable to endure the strain any further. His face and his whole body convulsed, as if the terrible admission were being ejected from his body in tangible form. Lavan, as well as all the other officers in the room, watched the hapless man's agony with pity. Then he sighed deeply, dropped his head on his chest and said in a low voice:

'I did it. I hid behind the curtain and plunged

the dagger into her bended back. May God have mercy on my soul.'

He shuddered violently and asked for a glass of water. Lavan muttered something and rubbed his forehead with his handkerchief. He looked almost as exhausted as Ferriter himself. There was tense silence until a man brought a jug of water and a glass. When Ferriter had drunk some water, he looked at Lavan and said:

'I admire your cleverness.'

Lavan was amazed at this remark. A minute before, the murderer had looked a pitiful wreck, his clothes fouled and disordered, his body limp, his face an awful picture of despair and suffering. Now he was transformed. He looked as solemn and as dignified as that morning, only more sombre and more insolent; like a weird hermit of the desert, grown ragged and unkempt and strange in mind through long privation and contemplation of forbidding mysteries, suspicious and contemptuous of his kind, already half dead, poised uncertainly between the known earth and the unknown eternity of death, indifferent to his fate. Lavan stared at him, wondering how the man whom he had in his power a minute ago had managed to escape.

'My God!' he thought. 'He's off again at

another tangent. I thought I had him at last and now he's off again.'

The murderer, however, removed his fears by saying:

'I say, you did this very cleverly, for I had meant to lie to you and fight it out, but I'm tired of the whole business. Now be quick and leave me in peace. What do you want to know?'

'That's better,' said Lavan. 'When you tell me your story I can help you.'

'I don't want your help,' said Ferriter. 'I merely want to answer your questions so as to be left in peace. Then you can do what you like with me. Do you think I'm a fool? You are in the habit of dealing with crude brutes, so you think I believe you. Not for one moment did I believe you, but I'm tired of the whole business. I'm tired because I no longer believe in the justice of what I have done. From the very moment I killed her I no longer believed that it was a holy act. Now I am certain that I have done a common murder. However, I stand alone. You want me to implicate others, simply for selfish motives. You want to incriminate other people like myself. I refuse. That manuscript was all rubbish. I wrote it after I had decided to kill her. I'll tell you the truth now.

Write it down and I'll sign it. The only favour I ask of you is to write it down exactly and not to change it afterwards.'

'It will be read to you before you sign it,' said Lavan. 'You can make any corrections you please.'

'Very well,' said Ferriter. 'I'm particular about this, because I feel that I'm going to be ill shortly. Are you ready?'

Lavan nodded. Ferriter coughed and then began in a loud, clear voice, with his head raised:

'I murdered Teresa Burke because I loved her and because I hated her lover, Dr. Michael O'Leary. I tried to rescue her from her profession, hoping that she would return my love out of gratitude. I was prevented from doing this by Dr. O'Leary. Having failed to ruin him by appealing to my society, I determined to kill him and get Teresa Burke convicted of the crime. I did not intend that she should be hanged. I meant to rescue her at the last moment and cause a sensation in the court by indicting the immorality of society. I would prove to her in that way that my love for her was noble and that she was an unworthy woman. I want to stress this point. What gave me the greatest satisfaction in the planning of the murder was the idea of causing a sensation. That is the truth. Write it down carefully. I wished to astonish humanity. Please let me see if you have that phrase written down exactly. I wanted to astonish humanity.'

'Continue your statement,' said Lavan. 'You may afterwards make any corrections you please.'

'Don't interrupt me,' said Ferriter arrogantly. 'I'll make this statement any way I please.'

He was now very excited.

'This was the most important motive behind this murder,' he continued, 'as the other motives were really subsidiary and accidental. I have suffered all my life from the mania of genius. Owing to my poor health, I was never able to do myself justice at school or at the university. Furthermore, I was persecuted by the other boys. That embittered me. It also made my health worse, as I brooded a lot. My relatives didn't understand me. There was no one in whom I could confide. When I had to give up studying for the bar after my father's death, I lost all hope of ever being able to express my genius in a normal way. It was then I began to think of doing something spectacular. It became increasingly imperative for me to force myself on the attention of the world. I shrank, however, from deciding on anything definite until I fell in love with Teresa.'

'Pardon me,' said Lavan. 'You forget your activities against immoral literature. Was not that part of your . . .'

'I refuse to implicate others to oblige you,' said Ferriter angrily. 'Why do you interrupt me? Please write down sergeant that I state on my solemn oath I was influenced by nobody in what I have done. You can't persuade me, Mr. Lavan, to implicate other young men that are as unfortunate as myself. What is it to me if they try to murder their sisters-in-law or become agents of the Soviet Government? All these people have been corrupted from infancy like myself. I want to indict the teachings of the Church, not these poor wretches who have been made the tools of dogma. I indict the Church you defend and the system of society you defend.'

'Very well,' said Lavan gently. 'Please continue your statement.'

The murderer had now become exalted, and he looked exceedingly ill.

'As to the other motives,' he continued, with a wave of his arm, 'they are easier for you to understand, especially my hatred of that man.

It was only by a vulgar chance that my hatred of him was connected with my love for Teresa. He represents most of the things I loathe in this life. He is a sensualist without intellect, a gross brute, uncivilized, without any refinement or sense of responsibility. He does not suffer in his soul but in his stomach, like a beast of the fields. Nature has given him all the riches she has denied me – bodily strength, healthy appetites, brute courage, the power to attract attention. I even envied him his crimes and his debaucheries. To injure him became an obsession with me, as soon as he laid hands on me that night and ever afterwards. Even now I loathe the man and I could gouge out his eyes. Write that down. I still hate him. It would have given me intense pleasure to have killed him, or to see him hang and dangle in the noose. But I lacked courage to kill him. He terrified me. I also saw that my killing him would arouse sympathy for him. I saw that it would be a greater punishment for him and for his relatives to have him convicted and hanged for the murder of a common prostitute. So I planned it in that way. I intended to wait until he was hanged. Then I would publish my manuscript and astonish the world.'

Here he smiled in such an extraordinary fashion that Lavan understood the meaning of the change that had taken place in him. Smiling in a grotesque fashion, he continued:

'That he returned and took her from me at a moment when I had a chance of taking her for myself was merely an excuse for venting my hatred of his type on him in particular. He prevented me from doing something less spectacular than what I did afterwards. I meant to marry her and scandalize my relatives. My love for her was the least important motive of all. It kept coming in my way while I was planning the murder. It weakened me. I had to use a great deal of my strength in order to overcome it. Otherwise I would not have made the blunders that have led to my detection. However, I enjoyed killing her immensely. Take that down correctly. I went through the act of killing her practically every night for a month and each rehearsal gave me intense satisfaction. For the last few days, the dagger-thrust was hardly ever out of my mind. It all happened exactly as I planned it. I express no sorrow for the crime. I am very glad that I killed her. I had no other motive than those I have mentioned.'

When he stopped speaking, he looked slowly

around the room and then smiled. Lavan asked him several questions, all of which he answered in a calm voice and in a very reasonable manner, even though he had begun to shiver from head to foot during the latter part of the questioning. His voice was steady in spite of the shivering and he seemed to be quite indifferent to what he said. He smiled now and again, as the statement was read over to him and he made some corrections here and there. Then he took up the pen to sign his name.

'Do you mind if I add something in my own writing, Mr. Lavan?' he said.

'What do you want to add? Is it relevant to the murder?'

'It's very relevant. It's the most important part of my statement.'

'Why don't you dictate it to the sergeant?'

'Please allow me to write it myself if it's in order.'

'Go ahead, provided it's relevant.'

Then the murderer wrote shakily:

'By this confession I have proved to myself that in taking this life I was not inspired by cowardice, but that I finally made a gesture of complete revolt against a false idea of God, by destroying that which is considered most sacred and yet surviving. There is no God, but man has a divine destiny. It is the duty of each man to become God.'

Then he signed his name with a great flourish. 'Is that all finished now, Mr. Lavan?' he said.

Lavan nodded. The witnesses added their names.

'That's all now,' said Lavan.

'Very good,' said Ferriter. 'You are quite sure it can't be changed? It must go on record without any change, just as it stands?'

'That is so.'

'Then I am free at last,' cried the murderer.

He stretched his arms above his head and burst into a fit of maniacal laughter. Still laughing, he went quietly with them to his cell.

'Poor devil,' muttered Lavan. 'He has already paid the full penalty.'

CHAPTER XX

WHEN the cell door clanged and he was alone, entombed, he stretched out his arms in a gesture of longing and all that was sweet in life was shown to him on a sunlit peacock's tail, upraised in magnificent pride, with all the joyous passions there inscribed in shining colours. Then this trembling ecstasy vanished. He dropped his arms to his sides and began to walk around the walls, muttering to himself.

Now all was deadly calm within his mind. There was no sound, no memory, no feeling whatsoever except a vague sensation of having lost something precious. He glanced nervously from side to side, looking for this thing. He walked on tiptoe, afraid to make any noise with his feet.

The death-like calm increased, until it seemed to issue from the walls, to pour from the roof, to rise from the floor and press towards him, in a curtain of silence without substance, yet heavy and impenetrable, like the upper firmament, when man mounts into the solemn emptiness of space and the airless wastes become a wall that press upon his shrinking flesh, confuses thought, obstructs the will, until movement becomes impossible. He moved slower and slower, and at last stood still and stiff, rooted to the floor and waiting.

Then the peacock's tail flashed once more before his eyes and spreading out its glittering fan into a circle, spun round and round him endlessly, increasing its motion and extending until the cell walls disappeared and all the universe was filled with whirling colours. Now the silence became inhabited. He heard triumphant singing, and the surface of the whirling tail was crowded with shining white angels that flew past him, beckoning and making promises of great pleasure. But he waited, watching eagerly, until at last he saw Teresa pass. She alone did not sing or beckon to him, for she lay prone upon the tail, with a dagger protruding from the back of her blue kimono. And as she disappeared she cried out to him in a piercing shriek, asking him to pluck the dagger from her wound and release her from her agony. Then she vanished on the whirling tail, followed by the shining, white angels, who paid no attention to her shriek, but kept on singing triumphantly, beckoning to him and making promises of pleasure.

Then he stretched out his arms and shrieked:

'Teresa. Come to me. I want to tell you something.'

He plunged forward, trying to grasp the edge of the tail and mount on it, in order to pursue her. But he struck his head against the wall and then reeled backwards. Now the whirling tail disappeared and there was a loud crash. He felt himself sinking downwards into a vast circle, like an arena, from which innumerable corridors stretched on all sides.

'Teresa,' he shouted, as he began to run around the arena, halting at each corridor and peering down its gloomy passage. 'Where are you?'

In each corridor he saw a grave scholar, whispering as he stooped over a manuscript. Each scholar raised his head at the question and said in a grave whisper:

'There is no God, but man has a divine destiny.'

At last he found an empty corridor and a manuscript, over which he stooped and read in a grave whisper:

'There is no God, but man has a divine destiny.'

Suddenly Teresa dropped into the centre of

the arena, where she lay on her face, dressed in a blue silk kimono with white spots. A blood-stained dagger was sticking from her back. She asked them in a shriek to draw the dagger from her wound. The grave scholars, all of whom were exactly identical with himself, rushed out of their corridors, waving their manuscripts and crying in thunderous harmony:

'There is no God, but man has a divine destiny.'

Then two eyes appeared and asked them what was wrong, and they crept back into their corridors.

But again and again and again, for ever without end, she dropped into the centre of the arena and they rushed forth, waving their manuscripts and crying:

'There is no God, but man has a divine destiny.'